ISBN-10:0-9987309-0-4

ISBN-13:978-0-9987309-0-5

Dreams in Deadwood

Scripture quotations are from the King James Version of the Bible

Author's note: This is a work of fiction. All locations, characters, names, and actions are a product of the author's overactive imagination. Any resemblance, however subtle, to living persons or actual places and events are coincidental.

Dreams in
Deadwood

Seven Brides of South Dakota

KARI TRUMBO

I dedicate this book to the writers who have helped me so much along the way; Melissa, Kit, Stephanie, Annie, Vivi, Lynn, just to name a few. I always thought writing was a solitary venture, until I put pen to paper and realized that I'd be nowhere without the friends I hold so dear.

Chapter One

J ennie smelled a change on the air as she peered out the back of the covered wagon at the slowly passing spindly trees. Her ma had always said she had a weird sense about coming danger. If only she knew better how to predict it, but it was a fickle gift at best. Something or someone followed them, maybe not close enough for her to see, but they were there nonetheless. She shivered as a bead of perspiration rolling down the back of her neck reminded her they were out in the open, easy prey.

She'd turned eighteen just a few days before, or was it a week? She'd lost count of the days. Her older sister, Ruby, drove their wagon and Ruby's husband Beau drove the other; there hadn't been room for all nine of them to ride in one. Her mother had stayed behind in Cutter's Creek and Jennie was still sore about it. She searched the trees one last time for a sight of anything moving, but the feeling had now dissipated to a low tingle in her blood.

They stopped to camp for the night and as they prepared and ate their supper, they listened to the old circuit preacher, Reverend Level, tell them stories of the Wild West. He was the one leading them to Deadwood, South Dakota. Jennie had been ignoring the tales for the last week or more. They hadn't even reached Deadwood and she already hated it, had a feeling deep down within her that it couldn't be a good place, not for her or her sisters. Nothing about this trip had been her idea. She'd have stayed back in Cutter's Creek if she could've. But, Ma had told her to go, told her to watch her sisters. So, she'd obeyed. She always obeyed.

The campfire burned down and Ruby led the smaller children to one of the wagons and got them tucked in on the feather tick in the back. She and her two younger sisters, Hattie and Eva, the twins, would share the tick in the other wagon. Sometimes Ruby joined them, sometimes not. She didn't speculate where Ruby slept the other nights, it wasn't any of her business.

Jennie climbed in the back of the

wagon and pushed Hattie over a bit so she had room to squeeze in. Hattie swatted at her hand and mumbled something, but rolled closer to Eva. It was a wonder how people could travel all across the country in one of these. She'd probably die first. It was hard work for those doing the leading or driving, or even walking, but for those just riding, it was dull.

A prick of fear had her sitting up and listening. Coyotes sliced the silence with a high-pitched sound; half bark, half howl. Then came the crack of a twig in the distance, and she held her breath, listening. The rumble of Beau's voice interrupted the cry of the coyotes and she strained to hear what he was saying.

An unfamiliar man's voice said, "Been walking for some time. My horse went lame a while back and I lost him a few days ago. I'm trying to get to Deadwood."

Beau answered. "Let me stoke the fire for you. We're pert near full up on seats, but the preacher we're trailing's got room in his cart, if you don't mind listening to him talk. You'll have to ask him in the morning. He's early to bed and early to rise."

"I'd listen to *spooks* if it meant I could get off my dogs for a bit." The man's voice was scratchy, like he was old or had sat by a fire too long.

Beau laughed and Jennie heard them move to where the fire had been between the wagons. Jennie crawled to the opening of the canvas and peered out, avoiding her sisters, and watched Beau and the stranger from the shadows careful to keep her fingers from view. The stranger looked blonde, though it was hard to tell in firelight. As he took off his hat she gasped at his ragged face. It was buried beneath a thick beard and smattered with dirt. He could be young, or old, it was difficult to tell. His clothes were quite worn and dirty, but they fit him well and the saddle he carried was made of a good leather, she could see the shine of it in the firelight. He had to have been strong to carry it for so long.

"Where'd you come from?" Beau asked. His stance wasn't necessarily welcoming. While he'd offered the stranger use of their fire, he also rested his hands on his hips, close to the gun always on his belt.

"California. Tried my hand at the pan and lost everything. Heard there's a mine in Deadwood that's hit it big and looking for help. Maybe, if I can't find a spot, I'll head over to Keystone or Hill City."

"You go ahead and warm yourself by the fire, the coffee's cold now, but it'll heat up fast."

Jennie gasped and backed further

into the shadows as Beau strode toward her, she didn't want to be caught listening. He veered off to the other wagon and rummaged quietly in the back, returning to the fire with his find. Jennie inched back to the opening, moving carefully over her sisters' feet so she didn't wake either of them.

"Here's a bit of tack. It's all I can find in the dark and I don't want to wake the girls. You can bed down under that wagon." He pointed right at Jennie.

"Thank you, kindly. I'm Aiden Bradly, by the by."

"Beau Rockford, and you're welcome to stay, just steer clear of my girls." His hand moved ever so slightly south and rested on the butt of his gun.

Jennie heard the slight threat in Beau's voice and shivered. For some reason, now that she saw the stranger she'd felt coming earlier, he didn't bother her a bit. Though he was set to sleep right beneath her, he'd be below her and could do nothing. She crawled back to her spot and pulled the covers around her ears, cuddling in closer to Hattie. The morning would come soon enough and then she could see what this Aiden really looked like. Man...or beast.

Aiden stared into the fire and toed off his boots. It wasn't near warm enough to go without, but he'd been walking for days straight and his feet were tender where the blisters had broken, then the boot had rubbed the sensitive new skin raw. He was happy for the smell of the pine wood as it burned, covering the stink wafting from his feet. He'd learned that if he could get them clean, then dry, he'd be fine by morning. But he'd need new boots before long and his money clip was looking pretty lean.

Beau had left him a cup, indicated where the wash water was, and then turned in for the night. He didn't intend to stay up too long either, but he had to attend to a few things or he wouldn't be much help to this family in the morning. He drank a little of the lukewarm coffee and let it sit in his mouth as he took a bite of tack. It was the only way to soften it enough to chew but his stomach was grateful. He'd had to abandon most of his provisions when he lost his horse. Taking only what he could carry.

He glanced behind him at the two large covered wagons and wondered just how many *girls* Beau had. He said a prayer that he hadn't come upon one of the wagon trains he'd heard about back in the Rockies, cat wagons, where women were brought in by the cart full to work in the brothels or sometimes stayed in the wagon as a moving brothel. That couldn't be it though, Beau had mentioned a preacher...hadn't he? Aiden shook his head. He couldn't remember what month it was. He was just happy to remember Beau's name.

Finishing the bit of tack, he plunged the cup in the wash water and carried it back to his seat by the fire so he could see what he was doing. He washed his sore feet, then bound them with two bandanas from the pack he'd carried. He carefully banked the fire and limped over to the wagon Beau had indicated. Laying his saddle down as a pillow and his blanket to cushion the ground, he curled up as tightly as he could to keep warm, and fell sound asleep.

Chapter Two

Jennie's eyes flew open and she held her breath. Something wasn't right, but she couldn't place what it was. She glanced next to her and clutched the blanket at her neck. Both Hattie and Eva were still fast asleep and it was still quite dark beneath the canvas of the wagon. In the distance, she heard Reverend Level whistling a hymn as he built the morning fire, but that wasn't what had woken her. She was used to his morning noise.

As she lay there it came to her: snoring. Deep, heavy snoring right under her. She crept to the end of the wagon, untied the canvas so she could slip open the back, released the bolts holding the tongue up, and gingerly released it.

Careful not to catch her dress on the rough wood, she slid onto the tongue and peeked under the wagon. Her long braid slid down over her shoulder and hit the ground with a soft thud. He was curled in a ball and grass blocked her full view of the man lying there. Aiden. It hadn't been a dream. And he looked even hairier up close.

A giggle escaped her lips before she could think better of it. She slapped a hand over her mouth, losing her balance on the back of the wagon tongue. She tumbled out, landing with a snapping sound, and crumpling to the ground on her head and shoulder.

Aiden sat up with a start, slamming his head into the bottom of the wagon. "Tarnation! Who's out there?" He blinked, looking around with wide, sleepy eyes.

Jennie wished the grass in the hills was longer...so she could hide in it. She lay on her stomach, hoping he was too sleep-addled to see her.

"You ain't hiding from anyone, girl. What're you doing laying there staring at a man? It ain't right." He shook his head and wiped the sleep from his soft hazel eyes.

Jennie glared at him. "Well, sleeping under a lady's wagon ain't right, either." She sat up and crossed her arms.

He laughed. "If I see a lady, I'll be sure to ask before I sleep under her wagon." He rolled back onto his pack and began snoring again, almost immediately.

Insufferable man! Jennie rubbed her head then climbed back into the wagon and secured the tongue in place. She was now wide awake, might as well help the reverend if he needed it. If she stayed, she'd just wake up her sisters, if the man's infernal snoring didn't wake them first.

Since all their belongings had been lost in a fire, Ruby had found each of them two dresses and one nightgown. Jennie chose her blue dress because it went the best with her eyes. She only took her braid out on bathing days, and they wouldn't stop for a bath for at least another few days, so she didn't worry about her hair.

She climbed out the front of the wagon, over the seat and down the wheel, sneaking a glance at Aiden as she walked toward the reverend. Men were, frankly, a rare sight and this one wasn't much to speak of with his reddish, shaggy beard and scruffy hair.

"Good morning, sir," she called quietly.

The short reverend with his bushy shock of white hair poked his head around the side of his small cart. "Good morning, child. I don't usually see you about this early. Was I too loud this morning?"

"No, sir. The man sleeping under my wagon snores." Her father had done that, especially after a binge of testing his own whiskey. She hoped Aiden wasn't anything like her father, especially about the drinking. Beau would have him gone in a jiffy if he did. Her sister, Ruby didn't abide alcohol, which meant neither did Beau.

"Is that a knot on your forehead? What'd you do, hit it on the side of the wagon?" He approached her and touched her forehead gently, his kindly old, gray eyes inspecting her head.

She flinched, not realizing how bad it hurt until that moment.

"You'll have to ask Ruby if she has anything for that, it'll bruise up fast." His brow furrowed and he tapped his chin. "You must've really hit it hard."

Jennie covered the spot with her hand and closed her eyes. How could she hide that from everyone?

"Hmm," the preacher mumbled. "Let me see what I have here. Don't think I've ever seen you girls wearing bonnets, but I think I might have one somewhere here... I often meet up with poor, young girls in my travels. Sometimes, they are so poor they can't afford anything. A new bonnet brings a smile to their faces." He stood up straight and smiled. "And sometimes, it makes their parents a little more likely to listen." He turned

17

and fiddled in the back of his wagon, moving things around, finally pulling something free. "Here's one that might work!" He handed her a cream-colored bonnet made for a child. She pulled it on and tied it under her chin, looking up at him and praying she didn't look as silly as she felt.

"Well, it doesn't hide it completely, you'll still need to ask Ruby if she has a remedy." He nodded. "Want a cup of coffee?"

Jennie nodded. "Thank you, sir." She sat by the fire and rubbed her hands together, waiting for the reverend to return from behind his cart.

"I get the inkling you aren't pleased about coming on this trip." He sat next to her on a stool and handed her a cup, then took a deep sniff of his coffee.

"You *inkled* right. I'd rather have stayed in Cutter's Creek with Ma. I miss her. I'll probably never see her again." Jennie shifted her feet closer to the fire, a deep yearning for home felt like a hole the size of the hills inside her.

Reverend Level laughed. "From what Beau told me, she was rather taken with a man named Carlton Williams."

Jennie shook her head and sighed. "She said there was a better chance for me to find a good husband here than in Montana. But that's foolish. There's even less people in Dakota than there is in Montana. She just wanted me to keep an eye on the little's is all."

"I don't think your ma lied to you. I think she *does* believe you'll have more choices in Deadwood. They run mighty low on good women there."

"It sounds to me like they run just as low on good men. Gambling, drinking...and all that other stuff that comes with it. I left a good little town to go to a den of demons." She clutched the coffee tighter to keep from shivering at the daytime thought of the things that had been keeping her awake some nights.

"Now, now. Don't think that way. Deadwood might have its fair share of trouble, but any new town will. Goodness, Dakota only became a state in '89, just three years ago. Everything's new in South Dakota."

"Except the Indians."

He chuckled mirthlessly. "Well, yes, there's that. But you've got to remember we've been buying up land they used to hunt on. If someone came by your house and moved into your garden, you'd be hopping mad, too."

Reverend Level stood up and stretched onto his toes. "I've used those grounds twice; you can toss them when you're done. I need to take my morning stroll and have some time with the Lord. Best make some noise to wake your crew. I'll be clicking out when I get back."

Jennie nodded and tossed what was left in her cup into the bushes. She turned to see Ruby just emerging from under the wagon, Beau right behind her, his hand possessively on her hip. Both were in the same clothes as the day before but something about that scene was too intimate for Jennie and she turned away, her face flaming hot. How Ruby could allow a man's touch after watching their parents and after what she'd been through before finding Beau, well, the thoughts couldn't be borne.

Jennie cleaned up the preacher's camp then went to help Ruby, Hattie, and Eva with their own. She caught Ruby's attention, who then strode up to her, narrowing her eyes, and tugged the bonnet off her head.

"Girl. What did you do to your head?" Ruby reached for Jennie's forehead, but Jennie stepped back out of reach, but not out of sight.

Jennie yanked the bonnet back up, but too late, Aiden joined the growing crowd standing around the ashes of last night's fire. Heat crept up her neck.

Aiden laughed. "She took a dive out of the wagon this morning and hit her head."

She wanted to stomp his foot, but she'd have to move to do it. Oh, she'd get him. Ruby pulled the bonnet back a little.

"I'm afraid I have no ice to bring down the swelling." She gingerly touched the raised knot. "It's hot to the touch, too. What happened, did you have a dizzy spell?"

Jennie shook her head and left the group to go help the littlest ones get ready. She heard more laughing, mostly Aiden, and her cheeks flamed again. That man was fast becoming a nightmare. Perhaps her initial feelings of worry were correct.

Frances, Lula, Nora, and Daisy all grumbled as Jennie pulled on their dresses and checked their braids. She could smell the smoke of the fire and knew the simple breakfast of biscuits and honey would be done soon. It wasn't a normal biscuit because they had no butter or milk, but they'd never had those things when they'd lived with Ma and Pa in Yellow Medicine, either.

If Pa had lived, he'd have married her off by now, probably to a drunk, just like he did to Ruby. Except Ruby had managed to get away and find a good man, a man who treated her like a prize.

She helped the younger girls get their food and did her best to stay far away from Aiden and his foul teasing. Beau laid his hand on her shoulder as she did the breakfast dishes.

"We're pulling out in a bit. I'm checking the wheels and straps to make sure everything's in shape for a good go today. Mr. Bradly offered to drive the second wagon so Ruby can ride beside me. I know she could drive, but I'd rather she not have to."

Jennie flinched at the thought of the scruffy stranger joining them. "Are you sure he can be trusted? He just showed up and you've invited him to join us? He could be anybody."

Beau smiled and slid his plate in the water. "He could be anybody, or somebody. I guess we'll just have to find out."

Beau strode away and Jennie shook her head. "He could also be a snoring jack mule that laughs when he shouldn't." She picked up a plate to scrub it as another plopped down in the water, splashing her. She looked up to see Aiden's hazel eyes twinkling at her.

"Jack mule, now that's a new one." He tipped his hat to her and turned away. She noticed he limped slightly and the ire melted out of her. According to him, he'd been walking for days and he'd been helpful that morning with Beau and Ruby. If he drove, her sister wouldn't need to, though, that also meant that she would be riding with him all day. When Ruby drove, Jennie would sit up front with her to help pass the time, now she couldn't do that. She'd have to sit in the back and listen to

Hattie's snipping and Eva trying to placate her.

Jennie herded the youngest ones to the wagon Beau and Ruby would drive, then climbed into hers. She laid on the feather tick and looked at the dark soiled canvas above her. The ride would be even more dull today since she couldn't sew or do anything else, the rocking of the wagon wouldn't allow it. Beau worried about Indians, so she couldn't even get out and walk.

"Hey, lumpy! Why don't you come up here and keep me company?" Aiden glanced back at her through the opening in the canvas.

She groaned and closed her eyes, pretending to ignore him. Oh, how every word from his mouth made her chafe. Even being bored would be better than riding next to him.

"Hattie, is your sister hard of hearing?" He laughed. "I ain't sitting that far away."

Hattie laughed and leaned close to Aiden, propping her arms on the short back of the wagon seat. "She heard you, she's just pretending she didn't. I'd sit up there with you."

Aiden threw back his head and laughed, she could admit, though she'd deny it, he did have a nice laugh, full, like a man's laugh should be.

"Sorry, sprout. You're a little young to sit up here with me, not that she's much older, I'd wager." He glanced at her again, a mischievous twinkle in his eyes.

Hattie turned around and sat with her back to him. "*She's* just turned eighteen."

"Well, that's practically an old maid in these parts." He patted the seat next to him as if he knew she were watching. Her ire rose even more. How could he tell?

Jennie sat up, then stood, bracing herself on the bows holding the canvas against the rocking of the wagon, then stomped to the front. She climbed over her sister and onto the seat, sitting as far away from Aiden as she could manage. Impossible man, why couldn't he just leave her alone?

"There, I'm here. Will you stop talking about me now?" She fixed him with a hot glare.

"That bonnet don't quite hide the knot on your head." He glanced at her head then back to the path. "The whole one side of your head's all purple."

If that was how he was going to treat her, then she'd get him just as good. "And your boots don't quite cover the stink of your feet, either." She gripped the side of the seat and turned away.

"No, I expect not. Guess we're both a sight." He flicked the lines.

"I didn't say anything about sight...

I said they stink."

"I did the best I could with the bit of water I had. Didn't want to soak them in the dish water." He glanced at her and there was that twinkle back in his eyes. She couldn't tell if he was pulling her leg or not.

"You wouldn't really...?" She turned toward him her stomach turning at the thought of him putting his feet in their wash basin.

"Why, course not!" He laughed, softening his face to pleasant hills and valleys, plunging into the hairy mass of his beard. A beard that looked out of place with his eyes, which were without lines. He had to be younger than she'd assumed the night before when he'd wandered into camp.

Jennie shook her head. He was a maddening man and she'd not let him get any closer.

He put the lines in his left hand and reached over with his right, tugging on her braid. "I thought plaits were for young girls. I ain't ever seen an eighteen-year-old wear plaits."

"Are you going to poke fun at everything about me? How about my nose, does that suit you, Mr. Bradly?" Her hands shook. How did this stranger make her so angry without even trying? She'd always been somewhat forgiving and placid, but every word he spoke made her want to stand up and throttle him.

"Now, that you mention it. Your nose is right pretty." He nodded as if the decision was final on the matter, which made her fume darkly.

Jennie stood and climbed back into the wagon, finished with him, at least for a while. If she stayed in the front, she was libel to push him off the seat and wave to him as she left him, and his beard, in the dust.

Chapter Three

Aiden watched as Jennie abandoned her seat. She was a feisty one, so much fun to rile up, just like Da used to do with Mam years before. He, his two brothers, and one sister had all worked hard on the farm, but there had always been moments of fun. Teasing was how they'd shown affection.

As he'd gotten older, it had taken more than teasing to keep him happy. He'd wanted something more than just silly words to cover up work worn hearts. He wanted to provide for his family, so they didn't have to work their fingers to the bone anymore.

A prospector had stopped at their farm on his way west. He'd convinced Aiden to leave home and come with him to find his fortune. They would strike it rich and he could come back and give his parents everything... Except that hadn't happened. He'd followed the old coot all the way to California, had worked and worked, and all they'd found was a few flakes. The prospector disappeared one night, the gold along with him.

California had left a bad taste in his mouth, but he'd heard if you could stand the cold and if you weren't afraid of Sioux aggression, there was gold in the Dakotas. He'd fair laughed at that. What would the Sioux want with him? The prospector had taken everything but his horse and his saddle. He didn't really want to fight Indians for anything and he suspected if he left them alone, they'd do the same. But, if he wanted to ever have anything to bring back home to his Da, he'd better get there and give it a try.

Though he didn't put much stock in *gold fever*, he could feel they were getting close to Deadwood. Deep down in his soul, he could tell there was something special about Dakota. It felt like he was right up in the clouds as he drove over the hills, then the hills had become steep and hard to cross. Some they'd had to try to stick to valleys, but the valleys seemed to become hills of their own, as if they were trying to keep

28

men away from their hidden treasure.

That morning, Beau had introduced him to each of the girls he'd mentioned the night before. He'd heard the story of how Beau and Ruby rescued the girls from unfortunate marriages. It was noble and all, and meant that the girls were safe to talk to, because they weren't free to marry. Which meant he could just be himself. He'd avoided taking a bride because his only passion was finding gold and making his da proud. Then, he could go home.

Aiden peeled his hat from his head and wiped the sweat from his brow. Though he was thankful to be off his feet, sitting in front of the wagon put him right in the burning sun. At least there was real heat. California had been cool and wet on the mountains. He smacked his lips and felt the cracks along the edges. A dipper of water appeared by his head. He glanced over his shoulder to find Jennie and her lavender eyes standing behind him, and he wondered how long she'd been there while he reminisced about times best left in the past.

"I thought you might like to wet your whistle." She hung her head and held out the dipper.

He wound the lines around his leg then took the dipper and drank deeply. He could have taken about three, but he didn't want to be greedy.

"Thank you. I was mighty parched." Her eyes brightened and she tipped her head as he picked up the lines again.

She took the dipper back then appeared near his shoulder again. Her skirt brushed against his back.

"Sure is hot today." She moved away from him, like a tentative child when offered a piece of candy. There was a quiver in her voice, and as much fun as it was to tease, it bothered him that she was nervous around him.

"Yup, sure is. Probably best if you stay back there, might be a bit cooler out of the sun." He was hoping it would challenge her to do the exact opposite as was her habit so far. True to form, she climbed over the back of the seat and sat next to him, folding her small hands into her lap and swaying with the motion of the wagon.

"You like being contrary, don't you?"

Jennie shook her head. "I always do what I'm told. It's just *you* I don't listen to."

He snorted to keep from laughing. "I think we got off on the wrong foot... M'or head. I'm Aiden Bradly and I'm from Kansas. I moved to Cal-if-ornia when I was a young pup of just nineteen. I lived there for a year, then started my trip to South Dakota. What about you?" He focused on the lines and traces leading up from each ox, hoping that if he didn't

30

look at her, she might just stay and talk.

"I'm Jennie Annette Arnsby from Montana, and I've always lived there. My Pa burned our house down when I was seventeen and my sister came to get us so we'd have somewhere to live. We lived in Cutter's Creek all winter and lit out in the spring. My Ma stayed behind. I don't want to be here, but I was told to go. And, like I already told you, I do what I'm told."

"Except with me." He smiled and pulled up on the lines. Beau's wagon stopped ahead of them and Aiden looked forward to resting his arms and stretching his legs, too. But it also meant the fragile hold he had on conversation with the little butterfly would end quickly.

"You don't count. You ain't family." Jennie climbed down the wheel and jogged away.

It took every bit of resolve she had not to turn and look back at Aiden. She didn't want to know anything about him except that he made her as mad as a hornet every time he opened his mouth. Except this time. He hadn't teased her, he'd tried to start over. When he was teasing her, she could give it right back,

31

but when he was just talking ... it made her feel like her insides were quaking.

Jennie collected the girls and brought them to the front of the wagon, where she caught Beau and Ruby locked together in a kiss like she'd never seen before. She backed away, but her sister's giggles made Beau jump away from Ruby as if she were on fire. He turned as red as Ruby's hair.

Beau wiped his mouth with the back of a gloved hand and pointed off into the distance. "See the birch trees? There's a stream over there. You girls go over and get cleaned up. The men will go later once camp is set."

Jennie had enjoyed the few times they'd stopped to bathe in the past, but now she'd be taking a bath with Aiden just a few yards away. Her belly did a strange flip at the thought. He wasn't family. Neither was the reverend, but somehow, Aiden was different. She held out her hands and the girls took them and they headed back toward their wagon.

"Both your dresses are dirty. We can wash one of them while we bathe. If the sun dries them enough we can get both clean."

The girls nodded and ran back to the wagon to get their clothes. Jennie collected her own clothes and the soap. She stuck her head into the back of her wagon.

"Hattie? Eva? There's a river. We're to go down and get cleaned off first."

Hattie threw her book across the bed and glared at Jennie. "What is the matter with you?"

"I'm sure I don't know what you mean. Get your clothes and come on."

"Aiden's been trying all day to get you to talk to him and you've done nothing but give him trouble. If you think there'll be a bunch of good men to pick from in Dakota, you're wrong. You didn't listen to all the stories, but Level told us there are a lot of men in Deadwood that need the gentle hand of a woman. Best to take one you know will be good to you."

Jennie shook her head and glanced heavenward. "I know no such thing and men need help everywhere, Hattie. But now, you need to listen to what Beau said or you'll still be down there when the men go down to clean up."

"And why would I worry about that?"

Jennie felt the heat rush up her neck. Hattie had always acted the flirt. She turned and left Hattie to sit in the wagon. She'd come when she was ready.

There were thin white trees all along the river. Their leaves were small and made a wonderful rustling sound as the wind passed through them. The river made a pleasant soft noise that you didn't notice unless you really listened for it. Like a whisper. Ruby and the younger girls were already in their drawers and chemises, splashing in the water. Jennie ran to the edge and handed Ruby the soap. The faster they got the dresses washed, the faster they could lay them out to dry before they got themselves washed up.

The sun sparkled off the gently running water and glittered as the girls splashed one another. Jennie inched into the cold river and helped Ruby and Eva scrub the stains from the dresses. Hattie joined them a few minutes later, but didn't join in the fun. Soon, all eight dresses were hanging from low bushes and eight sisters lay in the sun to dry themselves. Jennie glanced over at Ruby and her gaze froze on Ruby's waistline.

She assumed her sister had continued to wear a corset, but now, quite visibly, Jennie could see she wasn't. She only wore the corset cover to make it look as if she still were.

"Ruby..." Jennie whispered, "are you in a family way?"

Ruby rested her hand on her stomach. "I'd rather wait a little longer to tell everyone, if you don't mind. Beau will need to buy me the special stays when we get to Deadwood." Ruby gave Jennie a conspiratorial wink.

Having a baby was a great thing,

Jennie couldn't figure why Ruby would want to keep it a secret. They grew up in a very small home, with only two bedrooms. Though most of the girls knew what happened when you were married, none would talk about it. The most affection they'd ever seen was between Beau and Ruby, and it still left them embarrassed. Ma and Pa had barely even touched in the out and open.

Curiosity got the better of Jennie and before she could stop it, the words tumbled from her mouth. "Ruby ... do you like being married?"

She opened her eyes and glanced at Jennie. "Why do you ask?"

"I don't know. Ma and Pa never seemed to like each other until everyone was abed at night. But you and Beau can't seem to get enough of each other."

"Well, I suppose that's true." She closed her eyes against the bright sun and smiled, her cheeks a warm pink under the heat of its rays.

"Why?" Jennie had to know. How could she ever find what Beau and Ruby had, and not what her Pa had expected of her?

"Beau and I want the same things. We want space and time with each other. We want to spend every minute together, and we want to make sure all you girls have choices you wouldn't have had before."

"So, love is just ... things in common?" Jennie wrinkled her nose and sat up, reaching for the brush to attack the snarls in her long blond hair. Love didn't sound like much fun, if that's all it was.

"It isn't just that, Jennie." Ruby sat up and grabbed the brush from her, motioning for her to turn around. She started brushing the ends gently. "I can't even explain it. It's like when he's around, I can face anything because together we're stronger than we are apart. Before Beau, I was afraid of so many things. Now, I know I can be strong, because he's by my side."

Jennie enjoyed the soft rhythm of Ruby brushing, but stopped her when she started separating it into strands for braiding.

"I want to try it a different way. Maybe, more like you. I'm only a year younger, it's probably time."

"I suppose, Ma tried to keep you looking younger hoping Pa would forget you were marrying age. Let me show you how to wrap it up." Ruby slowly brushed through her own hair, then wrapped it and twisted it until it was in a pretty knot at the nape of her neck, adding pins to keep it in place.

"I think I can manage that. Thank you, Ruby." She worked at her own hair while Ruby left to check the dresses.

Jennie struggled to get her hair the same, twisting and changing it when it didn't feel right. It wasn't as easy on the back of her own head as it had been to watch Ruby do it.

Hattie plopped down next to her. "If you aren't going to be nice to Aiden, I will. I'm not even two years younger than you, I'll be seventeen before the spring's gone."

Jennie shook her head. "Beau isn't going to approve of Aiden, not as young as you are. You can ask him if you want, but I heard him tell Aiden to stay away from us." She didn't have pins with her, so she wrapped her ribbon around the knotted hair and tied it, hoping it would stay up until she could get back and finish it. It was a way to get Hattie to leave her alone, by looking as if she were too busy to listen further, when really, she just didn't want to hear Hattie any longer.

Hattie pinched the fabric of her chemise and drawers to check if they were dry. "Well, I'll ask him, anyway. I'm not opposed to being married and he seems like a good man."

"You've known him for a half a day. How can you know if he's a good man or not?" Jennie narrowed her eyes at Hattie. She had Jennie's full attention now. Hattie had always been the only sister to be mildly excited, even from a young age, at the prospect of marrying one of Pa's clients. They'd always thought it was because she was too young to understand, but Jennie wasn't sure anymore. Hattie seemed to have a pretty good grasp of what went on between men and women and was excited at the prospect.

"He smiles a lot and treats Beau and the reverend with respect. That's all that matters, right? I can teach him the rest."

Beau's voice echoed through the trees "Are you ladies about done?"

All the younger girls shrieked and sat up covering their bodies with the petticoats nearest them. The older girls knew Beau would never get close enough to see them. "We'd like to wash up before it gets dark," he called.

Ruby answered. "We'll be back in just a bit." She stood and gathered the dresses from the bushes and helped each of the younger girls get dressed quickly. Nora and Lula fought over the brush and Ruby took it from them, admonishing them to behave.

"We need to hurry. I'll get your hair in order when we get back to the wagons. We need to make some supper so it'll be ready by the time the men come back."

They arrived at the camp to find all the wagons had been pulled in a rough circle, and Level's horse and their oxen had been unhitched and were tied to nearby trees. In all the days they had traveled, they had never unhitched during the day.

"What's going on, Ruby?" Francis reached out and took Jennie's hand. Change always made her nervous. Her sweet face wrinkled in worry.

"I'm sure I don't know. I've been down at the river, same as you."

Beau flipped his change of clothes over his shoulder as he strode toward them. Ruby held out the soap. He stopped and laid his hands on Lula's and Francis's shoulders.

"I talked to the reverend. We'll follow this river, Level says it's called Whitewood, all the way to Deadwood. It's only a few more hours away. Tomorrow will be our last day on the trail."

The girls jumped up and down while Ruby hugged Beau. Jennie kept moving. The journey would be at an end, and then what? Supposedly, there were a lot of men in Deadwood. Men outnumbered women there a full ten to one, which meant it was dangerous. Her Pa had also told her stories of Wild Bill Hickock and Calamity Jane, though she was pretty sure both were dead now.

Jennie's stomach tightened and she felt sickly. The town which had seemed so far away, she never considered they'd actually reach it. Now, it was on the horizon and she wasn't so sure she wanted the journey to end. Ruby moved toward her and touched her shoulder.

"You don't seem all that happy to be nearing home."

She stepped aside, out of Ruby's reach. "It isn't my home. I never wanted to leave. First you yanked me from Yellow Medicine and planted us all in Cutter's Creek. As soon as we met a few people and started feeling like we belonged, you yanked us out into this wilderness."

Ruby frowned and shook her head. "I don't think you'll find much in the way of wilderness in Deadwood. From what I hear, it's a bustling town, bigger than Cutter's Creek, for sure."

Jennie's breath came fast as she tried to hold back what she wanted to say to Ruby. What she'd wanted to say for over a month as they'd been traveling. The words tumbled from her mouth as she lost her control. "And that's what you want? A big town with a wild past? I don't want that and I don't want to be here."

Ruby crossed her arms over her chest and her mouth flattened. "I'm sorry you feel that way. I wish you'd have told us when we left over a month ago. You could've stayed behind."

A girl her age could not stomp her feet and it would do no good anyway, but her feet itched to show her anger.

"No, I couldn't. Ma wouldn't let me. She said there was nothing for me there and it wasn't good to break up sisters."

The lines on Ruby's face softened and she touched Jennie's arm gently. "She's right. You've been together for so long. Wouldn't you have been sad never seeing Hattie, Eva, Francis, Lula, Nora, and Daisy every day? Wouldn't even missing one bother you?"

An unstoppable tear streamed down her cheek. "I would've been able to see Ma."

Ruby sighed. "The railroad is growing. Deadwood has a thriving railway that probably could take you right back to Cutter's Creek if you just can't stand to be here, but won't you give it a try? For us?"

Jennie narrowed her eyes and set her jaw, yanking away from Ruby's touch. She would never understand. She'd wanted to come out here, to follow Beau wherever he went, but not her. "I will give it three months. If anything happens to me or my sisters, we're going back to Cutter's Creek, to Ma."

"And are you taking them? What if they want to stay?" Jennie could see the small blue vein on Ruby's forehead pump angrily.

"Why would they want to stay in a gambling shanty-town full of drunken miners and prostitutes?"

Ruby turned on her heel and strode

off to the wagon. Her shoulders were set and her pace furious. She hadn't meant to hurt Ruby, it was just that her life suddenly felt like it did when she was back with Ma and Pa in Yellow Medicine. Back when she feared every day, wondering what would happen next. Cutter's Creek had provided security and Jennie wanted that feeling back. Somehow, the prospect of Deadwood didn't feel as promising.

Chapter Four

Aiden tried not to watch Jennie who sat away from everyone else at supper, looking rather forlorn. Something had happened while he was at the river, something that got her in quite a fuss. The whole group finished eating and Ruby stood to put the water pot over the fire to heat for washing the dishes.

Aiden waited by the wash bin for Ruby to notice him. She turned to him and smiled, taking his plate and dunking it in the water.

"Ruby, I hate to ask, but I don't have a glass to use for shaving. I'm feeling mighty shaggy." He scratched his thick beard and wished he'd been able to get rid of it before meeting up with them.

"Do you have a glass I can use?"

Ruby smiled and glanced toward Jennie then back to Aiden. "Beau has the only one and I think he'll be using it soon, and there probably won't be enough light when he's done." She scrubbed at a pot then paused, glancing over her shoulder, once again, at Jennie. "Ma used to have Jennie shave Pa, she's quite good. I can ask her if you'd like? I'll be warming Beau's towel over the water for the dishes. I'm sure we have another towel we could heat."

Aiden felt his belly tighten. Exchanging words with Jennie was one thing, but if she was allowed to shave him, she might just cut him long, wide, and permanent.

"I'm not so sure that's a good idea, ma'am, but thanks all the same." He turned to sit. He'd teased her a bit too much to feel comfortable with her holding a blade anywhere near him, especially not at his neck.

"Oh, it really isn't a bother. Jennie! Come here, please."

He closed his eyes, knowing he was heading for a fight. All he wanted was to look a little less like a grizzly bear when they rolled into town.

He could see the apprehension in Jennie's eyes as she walked past him to Ruby.

"Yes, Ruby? What is it?"

44

"Mr. Bradly doesn't have a mirror to shave with. If I get him set up with a warm towel, can you give him a good shave?"

He stood and shoved his hands in his pockets. "It isn't any trouble. I can do it when Beau is done." He knew, even before turning toward the sun, he'd never make it. There was no more than an hour of good light left, probably less.

Jennie smiled and narrowed her eyes to mere slits. He swallowed the lump in his throat.

"Now, Mr. Bradly. There won't be near enough light by then. It's no trouble at all. Why don't you sit yourself down right here?" She pointed to a stool next to the wagon. The leather strop used for preparing the blade hung nearby. A steer waiting to be branded probably didn't feel any less fearful.

He shook his head and crawled under the wagon to get his saddle bag. He dug out his leather shaving kit. It contained his razor, cup, soap, stone, and brush. It could take a man a long time to learn how to use a straight edge and not end up a bloody mess. Did this tiny girl really know what she was doing? Did he have any choice but to find out the hard way?

He froze where he stood, his heart beating like a rabbit's. The side of Jennie's mouth lifted in a sardonic smile. She knew what she was putting him through and was enjoying every second of it. She took the kit from him and gently pushed against his chest, pressing him backward onto the stool.

He pushed against her hand with his chest as he tried to stand back up. "You know. I'm thinking the beard doesn't look that bad. Maybe I'll just wait and visit the barber when we reach Deadwood." Jennie wouldn't move and he wouldn't push her away, so he fell back onto the stool and against the wagon.

"Oh, this won't take but a few minutes, and you'll look like a new man, Mr. Bradly." She laid the hot towel over the side of his face and wrapped it so it covered everything but his nose.

"I'd be happy to take your dollar, though."

"A dollar!" The towel suffocated his voice, but he heard her laugh.

Then he heard it. The sound of the straight edge against the strop; each long, slick *schlick* chilled his blood. He hadn't teased her that bad, had he?

She came back and massaged the towel into his cheeks, then removed it. Then she took scissors to his beard, clipping it close. He kept his eyes trained on her, but wouldn't move to say a thing, and wouldn't let her know he held onto the stool for dear life.

When his beard was trimmed short, she brought over another hot towel and again draped it over his face. He knew in his head that this was the way of it. It took all these steps to get a good shave, but each step brought him to the edge of reason worrying over that blade, but more over that girl.

"I'll get your soap ready. Good thing you bathed earlier or I'd have had to pick birds out of it."

He wanted to laugh. If she were in his shoes, he'd be doing the same thing, but he couldn't quite find his humor.

He heard Ruby finish up the dishes and there was the sound of that strop again.

That has to be Beau...

Beau laughed. "Look at you, getting the treatment. I couldn't get Ruby to give me a shave... not sure I'd trust her to." He laughed then there was a loud *thwack*— "Ouch! Why'd ya hit me for?" Beau yelled and laughed. Aiden heard shuffling all around him as if Beau or Ruby were chasing each other about the camp.

The towel once again disappeared from his face and lavender eyes appeared before him. Jennie stood over him and tilted his head back, then left to right, inspecting him. His neck felt mighty exposed. She tucked the warm towel around his neck and worked the lather in the cup with the wet bristle brush. She rubbed the soap on in deft circles, massaging his face even more.

47

He may have enjoyed it had it been the barber, but this girl ... he barely knew her.

She flexed her pretty lips into a frown as she hovered over him, pulling on parts of his face. Her body lightly pressed against him as she pulled the skin near his ear taut. It was the first time he'd ever wanted to back away from a pretty woman.

She stood up straight. "Now, I need you to lay your head back and open your mouth like you're a drunk, sleeping."

He blinked at her. Could she possibly be serious?

She pushed his head back a little further, forcing his mouth open, leaning the back of his head against the wagon. "Now, relax. I've done this more times than I can count and I never bloodied my Pa."

He sat up. "Are you sure about this. Really. I'm happy with the trim."

She pushed him back against the wagon. "Shush now. I need to concentrate. We've got to get this done while we have good light and I've never done this on someone sober, so sit drunk."

He complied and tilted his head back as she asked. She pulled the top of his cheek up with one hand and he held his breath as he heard the crackle of the blade cutting the hair. She bit at her lip as she did short strokes down his face.

He let himself take a breath as she lathered him back up for the second pass. He forced himself to watch her face and not think about what she was doing to him. She sure was pretty when she nibbled on her lip like that, though.

The angles of her cheeks were stark, as if she hadn't eaten enough, though they were just beginning to flesh out a bit. She was slender and delicate, especially in the hands. Her golden hair was the color of ripe wheat and now that he'd teased her about her plaits, which he'd liked, she wore it back in a standard womanly bun. Her eyes were almost lavender, the color of some lilies his mam had had in her garden. Her figure, he couldn't much tell. Her dress hung loose about her, as if it had originally been made for someone stouter.

Finally, she took to his neck, which had been the part he'd dreaded the most. He couldn't make himself think about anything beyond the scrape of each pass of the blade. He held his breath, and light-headedness threatened to take him down, but he fought it. After a few minutes, Jennie disappeared then came back with a basin of water.

"Here. You can splash this water on your face. It's cool."

He did as he was told and rinsed the heat and remaining suds off his face.

"Now. Let's see how I did." She stood in front of him and laid her hands on either of his cheeks. He reached up to pull them away. What was this girl doing, getting so close? He glanced up at her and saw something he never expected to, warmth. Jennie liked what she saw and he squared his shoulders, forcing a smile he hoped was less uncomfortable than he felt. He couldn't quite bring himself to remove her hands.

"Thank you, Jennie. I'm sorry I doubted."

She gently rubbed her thumbs over the top of his cheeks and he closed his eyes to enjoy the softness.

"That'll be two dollars."

He laughed. "That's a mighty expensive shave. Next time, I'll just wait for the barber." He dug in his money clip and pulled out two dollars, handing them to her.

She folded them and tucked them into a pocket of her skirt and turned away to clean up his shaving tools. Beau stood a few feet away, about half done with his task, and Ruby eyed him with a slight smile. He wasn't sure what to do with himself now. But it felt like he was the show just sitting there.

Little Daisy eased up to him and touched his knee. "Tell us a cowboy story?" She looked up at him with plaintive eyes almost the color of Jennie's.

He ruffled her hair. The sweet child

had his heart already. "I'm sorry, little one. I'm no cowboy. I'm a prospector by trade and those are no stories for little ears."

Jennie met his gaze as she turned from rinsing his brush. "If it's such a dastardly profession, why do you choose to do it, Mr. Bradly?"

She had him there. What could he say? The fact was, mining wasn't what he wanted to do, but what else could he do that would make enough money to keep the promise he'd made to his family when he'd left?

"Sometimes a man does what he has to do so he doesn't break his word. If a man ain't worth his word, he ain't worth much."

He couldn't sit around the fire any longer. The questions brought up things he'd rather keep buried. Like how he'd been suckered and wasted a whole year. He couldn't go home empty handed. His da would never forgive him for leaving to find his fortune if he didn't at least bring something back with him.

Jennie watched as Aiden wandered away down to the river. She hadn't meant her question to sound so mean. She'd wanted to know more about him.

Shaving all that hair off his face had revealed handsome, young angled cheeks and a strong chin. Coupled with his clean face, it had transformed him from a miner who looked like he came from a shanty town, to a man who could run off with her desires, if she'd let him.

She hadn't been able to help herself when she'd finished. There was nothing quite as soft as a man's cheeks after proper application of the blade. Her Ma used to cup her Pa's cheeks just as she'd done to Aiden. She often wondered what her Ma thought about when she'd held his face like that. Now she knew. When a man's cheeks were as soft as butter, it brought all sorts of things to mind that made her pink around the edges. Ma had said there was nothing quite like kissing the cheek of a young man fresh after a shave. Now that she'd shaved someone other than her Pa, she could see it was the truth.

Jennie put Aiden's kit back in the leather bag he carried everything in and then she replaced it in Aiden's pack. She couldn't stop glancing at him off in the distance, sitting on a downed dead tree.

If she moved quickly, she could go apologize before dark. She'd have to be back to the wagon by sunset. "Ruby, do you mind if I wander for a minute?"

Ruby turned to the sun and

52

squinted, shielding her eyes. "Go ahead, but don't wander far, and thank you for helping Mr. Bradly."

Heat rushed up her neck. "It wasn't anything, and I got two dollars out of it."

She would do it again, too, even without the money. Her hands itched even now to feel his soft skin under her fingers, and knew it would never happen. She slowly made her way to him, sitting next to him on the dead log.

He didn't notice her presence, or if he did, his expression didn't change. He stared off across the field of grass that led to the river. She fidgeted with her sleeve as the sun plunged lower on the horizon.

Jennie sighed and paused as she gathered her courage. "I'm sorry if my question bothered you. I didn't mean for it to."

Aiden shook his head but didn't look at her. "I got bigger things on my mind than making people think I'm something. I've just got to mine enough so I can get home. It ain't like I want to do this forever."

"So you haven't been bitten by gold fever?" Jennie sat forward to look at him, but he glanced away from her. Her stomach fell at his refusal to meet her eyes.

"Maybe I did at first, but the fever has long since cooled. My Da said it would, but I figured if I worked hard and brought back a haul, it wouldn't matter."

If what his father said mattered so much, that made him honorable. The more she learned about him, the more Hattie seemed right, he was a good man. "So, you're hoping to strike it rich in Deadwood, then take your riches home. Where did you say home was again?"

"Kansas, and yes. I don't even want to be rich. Gold is twenty dollars an ounce right now. I wouldn't need much."

"Well, I hope you find what it is you're searching for in Deadwood. I'm scared pert near out of my hair to go there. It makes sense that you want to go, but everything I've heard about it scares me. What if..."

He held up a hand to stop her, but the harsh lines of his face would have done the job. "Don't start down the road of *what if*, Jennie. Live life as it happens. You can't sit there and worry about tomorrow or you'll make your worries come true."

"I try to have faith that things will work out just fine, but people get hurt. I've been through enough to know that Deadwood could bring back all the things that scare me to death, everything we left Montana for: strong drink and the drunks that come with it, being sold off to anyone who sees fit to ask..."

"You don't really think Beau and Ruby would do that to you, do you? I may not have been with you but a day, but I can't see them doing that."

"No, I don't. I think women are so rare they'd be a temptation to snatch right off the street."

He didn't look at her, but laid his heavy hand atop hers between them on the log, sending a pleasant shiver up her arm. "I think you've heard a few too many stories. Tomorrow you'll see the real Deadwood. Yes, it's a town in the west, and yes, there've been some amazing characters who've passed through, but that doesn't make a town what it is."

"I've told Ruby I'll stay for three months. If anything happens to me before then, I'm going back to Cutter's Creek."

He turned his hazel eyes on her. The heat of his gaze and his hand covering hers made her heart trip. She'd met men in Cutter's Creek, but most of them had been married. She dearly hoped that her thoughts didn't turn to pudding every time she was near one. Of course, if they didn't, that would mean Aiden was different, and she didn't really want to think about that, either.

He whispered into the twilight. "I hope you give it a chance, Jennie. Deadwood needs ladies to pretty the place up as much as any town." He pulled his hand from hers and she immediately wanted the contact back. He stood and walked off toward the river, leaving her feeling cold even in the warm May evening. Jennie didn't feel welcome to follow. He had to have some war going on in his mind to talk to her without the teasing that usually came with it. She almost wished for the teasing again, if it meant he'd hold his shoulders back and smile again.

As the evening wore on, a chill descended on the camp and a light drizzle fell. Jennie helped with the rushed camp cleanup. Once she was done, she put her foot up to climb into the wagon but paused. Under the wagon lay all of Aiden's things, but it was empty of the man himself. He hadn't returned yet and he had no blanket other than the horse blanket he used to lay on. If she didn't do something, he'd get sick from the cold and damp weather. She dug through her trunk and found the blanket her mother had knit for her over the winter. She'd kept it perfect and refused to use it, thinking keeping it nice would somehow keep her mother closer to her. Now, she laid it out over the thick wool blanket so he wouldn't be frozen in the misty evening air.

It was dark inside the wagon and wet outside of it. There was nothing to do besides sleep, which was what Hattie and Eva decided to do. Soon they were softly breathing, but Jennie couldn't. She sat up, listening for Aiden to return. Though it was now full dark, and something howled in the distance, Aiden didn't return. Reverend Level would tell her to pray about it so she clasped her hands and closed her eyes, but words wouldn't come. She'd never been one to talk to the Lord. Didn't even know if He would just listen to her. Perhaps if Level prayed, the Lord would hear?

Jennie climbed out over the tongue and picked her way around puddles to the reverend's wagon wishing she'd thought to grab a blanket to cover herself with. Beau stood at the corner of their other wagon, cradling his rifle in the crook of his arm, protecting it from the rain. Staring off in the direction Aiden had disappeared.

"Jennie, what're you doing out in this? You'll catch your death. Get back to the wagon and keep dry, now."

"But Beau, what about Mr. Bradly?" She swiped the rain from her eyes and searched the dark, hoping to see him. A coyote called in the distance and the sound was like running feet up her spine to the nape of her neck.

"I got Aiden's gear from under the wagon and gave it to Level. He doesn't have much room in there, but I can't have him staying with you three. It ain't right for you to be out here looking for him, either."

She didn't move. "Has he returned at all?" She clutched her arms, shivering. The early spring rain was bitter cold, but she just had to make sure he'd come back. He'd left after her remarks and her guilt was a heavy chain around her.

"I'm keeping an eye out for him. You go get in that wagon now, young lady. I'm not going to tell you again." He pointed the way as the rain picked up, dripping off the brim of his hat.

She scooted back toward her wagon so he would think she'd gone in, but she still needed to speak to the reverend. She couldn't possibly get more wet or cold than she already was. She'd have to be careful and speak quietly or Beau would hear her and then he'd be angry. She'd never tested him and really didn't know what he'd do if he weren't obeyed.

The reverend sat in the back of his wagon, just inside out of the rain, and he looked up when she peeked around the door of his wooden buggy. It was like a large wooden box on wheels.

His old white eyebrow raised in question. "To what do I owe this late visit, Miss Arnsby?"

She gasped, reminded that she shouldn't go calling anyone after dark, but especially not an unmarried man, even if he was old. "I'm sorry. Please forgive me. I just wanted to ask that you would pray for Mr. Bradly's safe return."

His other eyebrow rose to join the first. "I already have, but now my question for you is, why don't *you* just pray? Surely you know that your prayers are heard by the Father just as easily as my own?"

If she weren't frozen, she'd blush. She tried to keep her teeth from chattering to alert Beau. "I don't know much, I'm afraid."

He nodded and his eyes were sad. "Would that I'd given you a Bible instead of a bonnet. Come see me tomorrow, child, and we can make a good trade."

She nodded then turned around and went back the way she came to stay out of Beau's sight. She would have to change when she got into the wagon and pray it didn't wake up her sisters. Warming back up would take a long time, but what of Aiden? If he hadn't returned, he'd be freezing, soaked all the way to the skin. What would keep him away in this weather?

If you hadn't scolded him about mining, he wouldn't have left. She knew it was true right down to her toes. Sometimes an apology wasn't quite enough. She'd already been in a poor mood about Deadwood and she'd taken it out on Aiden, but how could she make it right?

A coyote howled again and Jennie quickened her pace to the wagon. She climbed up and changed quickly, her fingers shaking in the cold. He'd be all right, he had to be. She closed her eyes tightly and tried to keep from shivering. If she woke Hattie, she'd have to explain why she was all wet.

Okay, Level, here goes. *Lord, I don't know how to do this, so I'll just ask. Please keep Aiden safe and bring him back to the wagon train... Amen.*

Most of the prayers she'd heard had been a lot longer with thee's and thou's. Those words meant nothing to her, but she hoped it wasn't required to sound like that.

There came the barking of either a dog or coyote, and it came nearer, until she heard it within the camp. Her skin tingled a warning and she hid under the blankets. Then voices. First Beau and then Aiden. She smiled as her heart leapt. There wasn't much of night left, but now that he'd returned, she could relax.

She had just closed her eyes when something large hit the side of the wagon, swinging all the hanging dresses above her head in a great arc. A picture fell from the side of the wagon where it had been tacked up and Hattie and Eva screamed.

Chapter Five

Aiden struggled against the rope tied around the scraggly mutt's neck, but it was wet and slipped out of his grasp. He'd found the dog while wandering in the cedar scrub to clear his thoughts. The old yellow dog was tall, and came up to Aiden's knees. He was a scrapper and had no intention to mind. The mutt ran for Jennie's wagon and jumped toward the tool box on the side. He landed atop it and growled down at Aiden. A wave of screams erupted from inside and Aiden could imagine their terror. He hadn't considered when he'd found the mutt that it would be a danger to Beau and his girls.

The dog had to be under his control

before it hurt someone. Edging closer, he lunged for the rope, yanking the dog off the tool box. He tied it to the wheel and scrambled for the dinner bones Level had left by the ashes of the fire. They'd stayed long enough in that camp to hunt a little, so there were fresh meaty bones. It was only a few jack rabbits, but the dog was starving and would have the bones devoured quickly.

Aiden threw them at the dog and he snapped them up, not even allowing them to hit the ground, growling when Aiden stepped too close.

"Aiden, what have you brought back with you?" Beau stood behind him, his voice a low rumble, now without his rifle, his arms crossed over his chest. Aiden didn't need light to tell him Beau wasn't pleased about the addition. The rain dripped off them both as they faced each other and Aiden shivered, just noticing the biting cold.

"He was being followed by a pack of 'yotes. I helped him get free but he hasn't been especially thankful yet."

Beau gestured at the dog under his wagon. "And what do you hope to do with him? He's gone wild. Can't even get near him." Beau's face may have been hard to read in the dark, but his voice wasn't. He was doing just what Aiden would do if he had a passel of girls to look after; protect them.

62

He glanced back at the dog, now curled up in the center of the wagon, the only dry spot left. "He'll calm down. I think I'll call him Jack."

The dog lifted his head and stared at him, then leaned forward. His hackles rose and he growled a low rumble that shouldn't sound half as menacing as it did since the dog was near dead with hunger.

"Don't seem like he likes that name." Beau came alongside Aiden, and he knew he had to be strong. He'd been pushed around enough as a young man, but no more. Beau would respect him if he stood up, and respectfully did what he had to do.

"Maybe not, but that's what I'll name him. Thanks for bringing in my pack. I had no desire to sleep on a wet bed."

"You probably will, anyway. You're soaked and there's nowhere to change. Level's little cart is hardly big enough to change your mind, but it's dry."

"Much obliged." Aiden knocked lightly on the side of Reverend Level's rig, then climbed in. It *was* small, especially with everything hanging from the ceiling and walls, but he toed off his boots near the back and curled up on his wool blanket. Atop his saddlebag was a folded up knit blanket that was not his. He didn't want to get it wet, but it sure would be warmer than going without. He unrolled a measure of his bedroll and covered himself with it, then he pulled up the knit blanket.

The wind blew the pots and kettles above his head together, softly clanging and plinking above his head. The noise of the rain and the song of the pots lulled him to sleep.

It seemed like he'd just shut his eyes when Level shook his shoulder. "Good morrow, Mr. Bradly. Are you in need of anything?" he spoke out of the darkness, and Aiden blinked wildly to remember where he was and who spoke to him.

He took a deep breath and yawned, recognizing the reverend. "No, sir. Just trying to catch a few winks before the sun comes up."

"Men don't take long walks in the rain for no reason. Either they are compelled by duty, such as searching for a military foe or chores on a farm, or they are compelled by a negative spirit in their head. We have no farm, and are under no threat of military action, as far as I can tell. So, Mr. Bradly, what is weighing so heavily on you?"

Aiden sighed and scratched his temple. The reverend wasn't going to let him go back to sleep, as much as he wanted it. At least he cared enough to ask. "Sir, all I really want to do now, is sleep."

"So, after finding a lost dog out in the wild, you have now figured out all of your problems and you can rest easy? Oh, that life were that easy for me. Perhaps I should keep my own ears open for a dog."

Aiden inspected the pots and other oddities Reverend Level had hanging from the inside of the rig, but kept silent. Chasing a dog wasn't going to make him feel any better about what he'd done with his life so far, and he couldn't go home until he'd fixed it. The dog was lost and beaten up, just like him. He couldn't just leave it there to die.

He heard Jack yipping and his eyes flung open. Jennie was in that wagon and would be scared out of her wits. Had Beau told them about the dog or just gone off to bed? He hadn't even expected Beau to be out waiting for him when he'd returned to camp, though maybe he hadn't really been. He might have been watching for coyotes. They didn't generally go for prey they had to work too hard for, and didn't like people much, but it was never a good idea to take that for granted.

He listened hard for the sounds of fear in the night, but all he could hear were the distant yips of the coyotes and the occasional growl of his own Jack.

"If sleep is what you need this morning, I'll leave you until the sun is up, but I do want you to think about the demon chasing you, Mr. Bradly. If you don't douse it, it'll enflame you."

Aiden blinked up at the ceiling as Level climbed out of the rig to start his morning. Now, he had plenty to think about.

Jennie had never had a dog in her life and she was sure after this night, she'd never want one. Every time any one of the three of them moved, the dog laying under the wagon would growl, at least she hoped it was a dog. It sounded more like a wolf. She tried closing her eyes and just ignoring it, but the fierce sound kept her tossing until the light of dawn glowed around the wagon.

She grumbled as she dressed, then stuck her foot out the back of the wagon. The dog yapped and lunged at her ankle, clamping onto her skirts and yanking her hard. She screamed as she lost her grip and tumbled to the ground, hard. The dog barked and growled, it's hackles raised on its back.

"Jack, no!" Aiden ran at the dog as it sprang at her. Her heart raced and she gasped, covering her face as it latched onto her just below the elbow. Pain raced up her arm. She couldn't think, couldn't breathe. *I'm going to die.*

Weight like she'd never imagined landed on her. She heard herself scream and then the weight vanished. She pulled her legs up to her chest, covering herself as best she could. Her hands shook as she swallowed back tears.

There was a commotion, yelling, but what they said she couldn't hear distinctly. She felt a strange pounding in her head. The pain blocked her hearing, her vision, everything but the beat of her heart. Strong arms wrapped around her and lifted her off the ground as if she were a child, caring arms like she'd always dreamt of when she *had* been a child.

"I got you... He was tied... I never thought..." Aiden's voice drifted through the pain. She raised her head opening her eyes and they focused on him. His eyes raked over her, stalling on her arm. He set her down on the tongue of the wagon, still nestled against his chest. He tore the fabric from her wrist all the way to her shoulder. She shrieked in protest, but the damage was done.

Her head swam at the sight of the blood running over her arm. It wasn't much, he'd only bitten once, but she'd never really seen her own blood before. Ruby rushed toward her with a bucket of water. Ruby's pale face worried her and Jennie couldn't stop her breath from rushing ahead of her, making her head swim. She leaned against Aiden's strong chest to steady herself.

Ruby set down the pail at Aiden's feet. "It's cold. I didn't have a chance to even put it over the fire, but it's clean far as I can tell."

Beau came forward. "Why don't you let Ruby handle this? We should take care of that dog."

Aiden lifted her arm. "I learned a few things about doctoring from the prospector I was with in California. I'll get the dog tied closer to me as soon as I do this."

Beau took a step closer. "I don't think you catch my meaning, Aiden. Let Ruby handle this and get your hands off her."

Jennie wanted to wrap her good arm around Aiden, to hold him close. His strength had fortified her and now Beau was taking him away. She looked to Aiden for help and his eyes bore so much pain. He showed her how to hold her arm bent and then turned on his heel and left. She swallowed her protest, her words had done nothing but damage yesterday. She hadn't seen him return last night, hadn't been able to ask if he was all right. What if he just walked the rest of the way to Deadwood and she never saw him again?

"No!" Jennie yelled when Ruby touched her arm. "Aiden, don't go!"

He turned back toward her and

waved as he gathered his saddle and the dog's rope. She ignored Ruby as she watched him get gradually smaller.

"Looks like I'll be driving the wagon into Deadwood. I don't think Beau meant for him to leave. Something's been eating at Aiden since last night and I think Beau was a little sore about spending so much of the night waiting for him in the rain when he would've rather been in the wagon."

Jennie closed her eyes. His teasing had been in fun and now it was her fault he was gone. She'd known that beast was under her; it had kept her awake all night. She should've been more careful climbing out of the wagon.

"I know it's silly, but I'm going to miss him, Ruby."

"I know. Beau told me you came out to check on Aiden last night. Beau trusts him enough to let him travel with us, but I'm not so sure he thinks Aiden is good enough for you."

Jennie's heart clenched in protest. "That isn't his decision. I didn't go from letting Pa pick who I would marry to your husband doing it. *I* will decide. No one else. You said yourself yesterday that it was important to you. Was that a lie?"

Ruby avoided her question and her eyes. "You think there was marriage in your future? I didn't think you two were all that close. Heavens, it's only been a day."

"We weren't, not at all. I'm just saying it shouldn't be up to you or Beau or Pa or anyone else."

Ruby wrapped a bandage around Jennie's forearm and tied it near her elbow. "I don't think you'll have to worry. The bite was surprisingly shallow. I've never seen a man move so fast as Aiden when you screamed. I think he *flew* across the camp to get Jack off you."

Jennie looked down at the bandage running her hand down her arm and shivered. "Why did he bring that beast into our camp?"

Ruby collected the damp and soiled cloths. "I'm sure I don't know. He didn't say much to anyone when he came in last night. All we know is that he was late and he brought the dog with him. Beau said he got it away from some coyotes."

Jennie searched off into the distance, but he'd long since disappeared from view. Beau strode out from behind the other wagon, his face dark.

"We need to eat quickly, then get back on the trail. Level wants to be in Deadwood by the noon."

Ruby touched Jennie's knee. "Just rest back here. Hattie and Eva are enough help. One of the girls will bring you something to eat. I'll mend your sleeve later, after we wash the dress."

70

Jennie nodded, not really caring about any of it. She'd wanted her first experience of Deadwood to be with Aiden, since he'd been excited about their arrival. She'd thought he would somehow make the fear in the pit of her stomach go away. Now, she'd have to face Deadwood, alone.

Chapter Six

Aiden's feet swelled after just an hour of walking and he could go no further. "Jack, hold up. I've got to rest a bit."

The dog bounded back to him and sat a few feet away, cocking his head.

"Why'd you have to bite Jennie? If you had to get angry with anyone it should've been me. I'm the one who tied you up. She didn't do a thing."

Jack sat and stared at him, panting. "I don't have any rations, boy. You'll have to go off and hunt on your own and I guess I gotta hope you come back." He tugged the rope and Jack pulled on it. When he got Jack close enough, he untied it and Jack ran in circles, then laid down by his feet.

"Go. I know you need to eat. You're skin and bones. I'll be just fine." He peeled his boot off his foot and sucked in his breath as they throbbed. The oily stuff that had been coming out of his feet was thick and shiny in the sun, and the smell turned his stomach. He hadn't been able to take care of them the night before when he'd gotten back so late. "Doesn't look like I'll be going anywhere soon, boy."

The dog whimpered and inched closer.

"You didn't act this nice back at the camp. What was the trouble?"

He heard the sound of wagons approaching and hung his head. Beau was the last person he wanted to see. And Jennie would never want to see him after Jack had attacked her. How could he explain to her that Jack was like him? He'd been run off, abused, chased, starved, and finally just run. Jack needed him, and life was a little less hopeless if something needed him. Aiden glanced behind him toward the sound of the wheels against the rocks under the sparse grass. He didn't recognize it. It was an old buckboard with an ancient man tottering at the lines.

"Ho!" The old man yelled down. "Who goes there? Need a lift to town?"

"I do. Can my dog follow?" Aiden glanced up and winced as he shoved his foot back into his boot.

"Don't see why not. You headed to Deadwood? Looking for work?"

Aiden laughed as he climbed up and Jack jumped in the back, the old man didn't seem to notice or care. "Yes, and yes."

The old man held out his hand. "Boom's the name. I work with a small mining outfit in Deadwood, it's hard to get work on the big mine. Men don't want to leave once they git a spot. But our outfit finds pay dirt often enough to keep our few miners working."

Aiden nodded. "That's what I'm looking for. Are you sure they're hiring?"

The old man threw his head back and cackled. "Yup, cause it's my claim. Deadwood's about two hours away by this route, but I was out checking a few things in Preston, then at the big load in Lead. Good thing I happened by. It ain't a good idea to be walking out here alone. Deadwood's been a town for almost twenty years, but we still keep our eyes open. This *is* Indian country."

The man's condescension made him chafe. Everyone assumed that since he was young he didn't know anything. His da had been the same way. He'd never planned to be out walking alone, anyway. When he'd left his first claim back in California, he'd *planned* to stick to the stage coach trail, then his horse died. Then, he'd *planned* to stay near the river, until the river he'd been following dried up. He'd met up with the Rockford group later, but then he'd been a fool. Now, he knew what his problem had been, he shouldn't have been *planning* at all.

"You know, Boom, I think I was meant to meet up with you today. I'm Aiden Bradly, and I know gold and how to stir it from the earth."

"Good to hear, son. We don't want 'em green."

No one ever did.

Jennie sat next to Ruby as they pulled the wagons out of the circle and formed a line with Reverend Level in the lead, Beau following, and Ruby tagging behind. Jennie wouldn't miss the inside of the wagon one bit. She'd always thought sharing one room with her sisters growing up in the tiny house had been difficult, but it was nothing compared to the cramped covered wagon.

Jennie held her arm tight to her chest, every bounce and shifting of the wagon sent a fire up her arm. She watched the ever-changing horizon as they slowly climbed over swells and maneuvered through valleys. When she was sure she couldn't take the sight of another evergreen tree, a city grew up in front of them, squished between three tall hills and surrounded by deadfall.

Ruby pulled up on the lines and stood, shading her face. Jennie sat in awe and gasped, shading her eyes from the pressing sun. The town was made of *stone*. There wasn't a shanty in sight and no tents, either, it was a bustling city, bigger than Cutter's Creek and far larger than anything she'd ever seen.

"They made it of stone... like a castle from one of those stories you read us in Cutter's Creek." Jennie could hardly get the words past her throat. An excitement she hadn't expected built inside her. All the rocks were light colored and glinted back at her in the sunlight.

Ruby glanced at her, a twinkle in her eyes. "The city of Deadwood has had a lot of time to grow. You'd have known that if you'd have listened to Reverend Level instead of going off on your own deciding how much you hated the idea of coming here."

"I'm sorry now I didn't pay more attention." Jennie swallowed hard. "It isn't at all what I expected. What're we going to do once we get there?" Jennie gazed up at Ruby. Now that they were here, new worries attacked her. Where would they live? Did they have supplies? What if goods were more expensive?

Ruby handed Jennie the lines and stretched her back gingerly, then sat back down ready to catch up to Beau's wagon.

"The first thing Beau needs to do is get us lodging for a night at a boarding house or hotel. Then he'll need to find work so we can talk to the land office about housing. We had some money saved for the trip, but we didn't know how much land costs here. I'm not afraid to work. I've heard there are laundries and restaurants here, not just saloons, gambling houses, and other places we have no business talking about."

"I'm sure all of us are willing to work." Jennie glanced back at Hattie. Jennie had an inkling that Hattie, more than anyone, would be more willing to work *any* job. She shook off the feeling and prayed what she hoped was a proper prayer for forgiveness. Thinking such things about her own sister would only cause strife.

"I'm just not sure what work we'll find. Just keep your eyes open and pray for something to make itself known. Beau has always been good about finding work wherever he is, but that was when he was alone. Now, he needs work that'll provide for his whole family."

"I guess since Ma and Pa made do with so little, I never thought about what it costs to have a family, but I bet it was hard going from one man to a family of nine..."

Ruby smiled absentmindedly and flicked the lines, now in a hurry to get close to Beau's rig. "He's learned to trust less in himself and more on the Lord in these last few months. He's responsible for all of you and doesn't take that lightly. I'm sorry you felt he took your choice away from you when Aiden left. It wasn't his intention to make him leave. He just needed Aiden to understand, in the same way *he* had to learn, that you're all precious and take special care. He wants you to be able to turn to him like a father, without ever asking you call him that or forcing you to treat him as one."

Her heart lurched in her chest. Beau wanted to be a real father to her, so much more than the man who'd actually carried that title. "I never thought of it that way. I was thankful for you, and for him, but I never took account of what it cost both of you. What will you do when... I mean—" She glanced down to Ruby's waistline suddenly worried that when a baby came, they wouldn't want the burden of her or her sisters.

"We'll be a family of ten," Ruby whispered as she leaned in close and flicked the lines once more, the oxen powered ahead and Jennie groaned as the jolt jerked her back in her seat. As they navigated through the thoroughfare of people and animals, they had to slow way down as Ruby concentrated on avoiding everything with the heavy wagon.

They pulled their small train down the main street and stopped in front of an inn. Reverend Level and Beau climbed down stiffly and went inside The Grand Central Hotel, Jennie and all her sisters waited outside.

A handsome, younger man in a suit walked by and tipped his hat to Ruby and Jennie. The longer they sat in the street, the more men stopped and just stared at them.

She didn't see a single woman around them. So, at least some of her fears had been warranted. There were many men bustling about doing business and the city was huge, with many blocks of housing and businesses climbing up the face of the nearby hills, but she didn't spy a single swishing skirt.

The younger man approached their wagon and leaned against the buckboard.

"Hello ladies. Welcome to Deadwood. Name's Roy." He wore a smart gray suit and black satin string tie, with a light Stetson perched on his head, shading eyes just a little too beady to suit Jennie's taste.

Beau strode out of the hotel and stood next to Roy, shooting him a glance that would've had her moving fast had it been her in Roy's shoes. He elbowed his way to the wagon holding out his hand for Ruby. "I have a place for us, but let's get a little lunch, then I'll take you to the house we'll rent until we can get our own homestead."

He stepped back and looked at Roy. "Can I help you with something? Don't you have somewhere to be, mister?"

Roy held up his hand and stepped back. "No, no. I thought you were someone else entirely. Good day." He tipped his head and strode off.

Ruby let Beau help her down. "Strange fellow, though it seems we've attracted quite the notice."

Jennie scanned the street around them and some men were outright staring, while others tried to make it less obvious.

Ruby touched Beau's arm. "I don't think it's safe to leave all our things out here in the street. We should get all our belongings put away, and then get lunch. With all of us, it won't take long." Ruby sighed and glanced back up at the seat. "I was looking forward to a short break, but, with as busy as it is here, I'll do whatever you think is right, Beau."

"How about we compromise? The owner of the hotel has a small livery in the back and he said we could use it until we get ours cleaned out. I'll move the wagons back there while you ladies wait here."

Ruby shook her head. "If it's all the same to you, I've been kidnapped before and don't intend to let it happen again. We'll follow you, then go in the back of the inn"

Beau kissed her on the nose. "Sounds good, we'll get these moved then join the reverend inside."

Beau and Ruby maneuvered the wagons through the busy, crowded street, and around the block to the small stable in the back of the inn. Unlike out front, no one stood around to look at them back there.

Jennie laid down on the feather tick with the younger girls and waited for Beau to secure the oxen and give them some hay and water. She couldn't help but wonder what had happened to Aiden. She'd hoped they'd have caught up to him before reaching Deadwood, but they'd seen nothing of him. She'd wanted to apologize for Beau. Perhaps even convince him to stay, though maybe not his dog. They were both in Deadwood, but would they ever see each other again?

Beau called for them and they went into the inn to get lunch. When they'd finished, he walked them two blocks from the inn to a house the size of the one they'd left in Cutter's Creek. It had huge front windows, a wrap-around porch and enough room for all of them. Ruby and Beau walked arm-in-arm ahead of the group, smiling at one another.

"How did you get this for us? Why didn't the man at the inn just let us rent a room?"

"I explained to him that we'd be looking for a home and there were quite a few of us. He didn't really have the space for such a large family and for what could be more than a day, so he suggested this. It was his mother's home, but she passed recently and he hasn't had a chance to sell it, so he'll rent it to us until he can find someone."

"And do we intend to be that someone?" Ruby asked as they waited for him to open the door.

"I guess we'll wait and see what the inside looks like and how much they want to sell it for. If I can find a good job soon, it might be possible."

Beau pushed open the door and they entered onto gleaming wood floors that led to a large fireplace. On the other side of the room was a large dining area and a table with enough chairs for all of them. Along the right wall was a staircase that led to the second level where the bedrooms were. And along the back wall, behind the stairs, was the small but serviceable kitchen.

Ruby stood in the middle of the room and held her arms out wide, slowly spinning in a circle, smiling when she finally stopped. "It's perfect, Beau."

Jennie felt the same way. After living in the tiny confines of the wagon, a home where you could stretch your arms out wide and not touch anything was a blessing. Lula yelled from upstairs, "There's beds up here. Almost enough for all of us to have our own!"

Beau took Ruby in his arms and danced her around the large room. Jennie turned away from their affection.

"Will you work in the mines, Beau?" Jennie turned back toward the couple, her question stopping their celebration.

"I don't think so, Jennie. I've never worked in a mine before and it's dangerous work. The railroad is big here, I've done that, cattle work, worked with horses, and moving freight with ox carts. I'm sure I'll find something to do. I feel it, right down to my bones, this is where we belong." He smiled down at Ruby.

If only Jennie felt as sure.

Chapter Seven

Boom drove Aiden to the outskirts of Deadwood, then bypassed the town and went around to a small area with what seemed like endless rows of tiny decrepit homes. It was the shantytown Jennie had been so fearful of. The one he'd assured her didn't exist. It wasn't supposed to, at least that's what he'd heard. All along the edge of the shantytown was a row of houses painted red. He'd live in his very own red-light district without even being near the railroad. Aiden shivered. He hoped wherever Boom led him was far away from the cribs.

Boom pulled up in front of a shanty with a sagging roof and no paint. It looked only a little bigger than an outhouse. A foul smell surrounded him and he held the bile in his throat at bay. There was nowhere for the men to empty chamber pots or spittoons, and litter had piled up in public areas. Even at the California claim, he and the prospector had been neat. Looking about him now, it was a wonder they didn't all die of disease.

"The last guy that had this one didn't take such good care of it. It's got a cot, a stove, and a table. Don't need much else. I'll pick you up tomorrow morning, work starts early."

Aiden climbed down, grabbing his saddle from the back of the wagon, and keeping the pain in his feet barely under control. Jack jumped down, sitting by his feet and they watched as Boom turned his wagon and headed toward Deadwood in the distance. Aiden limped to the small run-down building. As he opened the door, he noticed there was no lock on it, or any way to keep people out. The bed was a nearly flat tick that had seen better days. He'd have to search for miles to find enough material to fill it. He pulled back the shredded curtain that covered the one crate on the wall for storing food and dishes. It held one dirty plate, cup, and bowl. There was no food, no kindling or wood for the stove, and he had no way to get into town except to walk. He didn't even have an ax to cut wood.

He glanced out at the sun. It was only around noon, but getting his new home in order would take most of the day. He knew it would take a few trips, but he grabbed a flour sack he found on the floor and called Jack to follow him.

Though there were a lot of trees, the ground was surprisingly free of twigs. Just under the sparse grass was a layer of rocky gravel, it was sparse and coarse, he wouldn't use it unless he had to.

Aiden searched in several areas about the camp, but came up with very little he could use, finally settling on the grass, the very stuff he'd hoped to avoid, hoping that as it dried in his mattress it wouldn't rot or get prickly. He brought the grass litter in and stuffed his tick full. When he'd finished, he was tired and his feet burned.

Peeling off his shoes once more, he noticed the odor which had bothered him before was now much worse and his sweat was not only oily, but thick. He shook his head and lay on his new bed looking up at his sagging, uneven roof. A prayer formed on his lips, a prayer that it wouldn't rain before he got a day to repair it. Then, he fell into a deep sleep.

His hand was wet, that was his first thought as he woke up to Jack licking him. It was dark in his little cabin and he sat up, looking out the window. All around him, shanties were lit up with men spilling out all over. Music and male banter reached him through his thin walls. He would never make it to town and back and he hadn't gotten wood or extra leaf litter and twigs for kindling. He rifled through his pack and found a few dollars. He hoped it would be enough for a meal in town and that he could find his way back out to his new home in the dark.

Every step he took sent pain further up his legs. Though he hadn't gone far, he rubbed the sweat from his brow and took off his coat. Had it been this hot when he'd arrived in Deadwood? It sure seemed warm now. He pressed on though his feet throbbed. With each step, he had to hold his breath, which meant he made nary any progress at all.

Jack whined and ran ahead, then scampered back for him, but as hard as Aiden tried, he couldn't go faster. Full night came and the trail became difficult to see. Aiden tried to lift his feet with every step, but they were like lead at the end of his legs. He tripped over a large stone on the side of the road and tumbled down the embankment into the ditch. Jack scampered down, licked his face, and ran off barking.

"I didn't leave *you!*" he yelled. His voice hoarse. He tried to pull himself up

87

but ferocious heat engulfed him. His body began to shake and he closed his eyes, collapsing in a heap.

"Stop fidgeting, Jennie. What's gotten into you this evening? This house is snug and safe as a bank, yet you're wringing your hands and pacing. You're making me nervous." Ruby planted her hands on her hips and glared at her.

Jennie couldn't explain it if she tried. Something had her wound tighter than Carlton William's clock back in Cutter's Creek. She'd checked that both doors were locked and looked through the whole house for what had her in a turmoil, but came up with nothing.

"I guess I'm just nervous to be in a new place, is all. I'm sure I'll settle down after a bit."

"You're going to open up the bite on your arm if you don't. If you can't help me here in the kitchen, go find something to do. I can't get anything done with you pacing about."

Jennie left the kitchen and went back up to the room she now shared with Hattie and Eva. The house was fully furnished, which was good, because they hadn't brought much with them. It wasn't a large room, but it didn't matter. The bed was big enough so she wouldn't be crowded, there was a desk to sit at, and she had a place to hang her dresses, if she ever had more than two. Jennie picked up the dress she'd changed out of and discarded on the floor. Aiden had ripped it right up the seam. The dress had been large on her anyway, so she could repair it using the extra fabric.

"Jennie! Come on down here!" Beau yelled from below.

Jennie tossed the dress on the edge of the bed and ran down the stairs, holding her skirts away from her flying feet. At the base of the stairs, she stopped and gasped. Jack sat at the front door waiting for Beau to open the screen and let him in. He whined pitifully and lifted a huge paw in the air, gently jabbing at the wood as if to knock.

"Jack... where's Aiden?" She glanced around the room, but he was not there.

Beau opened the door and allowed the scruffy dog inside. The mutt approached her slowly, and she sat on the stair, her heart racing in her ears. The dog laid his head in her lap and whined. She pulled back, but his soft brown eyes stopped her.

"You're sorry, eh? So, where is that

master of yours?" She gingerly laid her hand on the dog's head and he scooted closer, looking up at her.

"Aiden had gotten mighty attached to that dog after saving it. I don't think he'd leave our train for the dog, then let him go. I'll go with Jack and see if we can track him down." Beau opened the drop down of the secretary's desk by the door and grabbed his gun belt from inside, fastening it on. He pulled the gun from the belt and filled each chamber, then slid it back into place. Grabbing a few extra bullets, he put them in his leather munitions pouch.

"Come on, Jack. We need to find Aiden." Beau opened the door and the dog lifted his head off Jennie's lap. He nipped the bottom of her skirt and pulled.

"No boy, I can't go out there. But I'll be waiting right here when you bring him back." She patted his head. He whined and pulled again.

"Jack," Beau called and the dog reluctantly let go of Jennie's skirt.

She watched as the two disappeared into the night. Ruby locked the door behind them.

"I'm surprised you didn't hear the commotion. He started scraping on the door as soon as I sent you out of the kitchen. He must've tracked us by scent, because he couldn't have known we were here."

"He must've been a good dog for someone." Jennie replied. "Now, I hope he's a good dog for Aiden."

Ruby stood behind her and gently gripped her shoulders. Jennie realized she was shaking.

"Beau and Jack will find Aiden and bring him back here. Though with the way they parted, I don't know if Aiden will come here or not. Maybe you could make yourself busy cleaning up that servant's room down here behind the kitchen? That will give you something to focus on. Also, that'll be a good place for Aiden if he decides to stay. Far away from all of you." She peeked around Jennie's arm to the other girls in the parlor.

Jennie couldn't help the tear that ran down her cheek as she searched the darkness out the window, knowing Aiden wouldn't be found so quickly. "Or in case he has no choice..."

"Well, now, I wasn't going to say that, but we both know Aiden was having trouble with his feet and he walked a long way today. Beau wouldn't let me look at him, but from what he described to me, he might have some sort of infection." Ruby shook her head. "Men and their infernal ways. If I'd been able to look, I could've told him right away if they were just sore or if they needed tending to. I have to finish supper now or we'll never eat. You go get busy."

With Ruby's red hair and no-nonsense words, she reminded Jennie of Ma, so she didn't complain about being told what to do. Jennie stopped at a small linen cupboard and grabbed clean bedding, then opened the servant's room.

The house was equipped with room for one servant, not even a couple could fit in the small space. The bed was little bigger than a cot, but had a mattress stuffed with feathers so the lady must have cared for whomever had been doing her chores and cleaning. Jennie dusted the few pieces of furniture with a wet rag and made the bed. She'd added oil to the lamp and opened the window to let in a little air when she heard Jack barking again.

Jennie couldn't keep to the room and finish. Had Beau found Aiden? She ran out to the kitchen in time to see Hattie unlock the door. Jack raced into the house and skidded across the shiny floor. Beau struggled under the weight of an unconscious Aiden over his shoulder.

"Beau, the room is ready back here." She called and moved out of the way in the narrow passage leading to the back room. Beau shuffled past her and she heard a grunt and the moan of the ropes holding up the bed mattress as Beau dumped Aiden onto it. She peered through the door and saw Beau working to pull off Aiden's boots, but they wouldn't come off. Ruby pushed her aside as she bustled in with a pair of scissors.

"We've got to cut them off." Ruby knelt beside him.

"Ruby, I don't want you to have to do this." Beau refused to move and laid his hand on her shoulder.

She shook his hand off. "Beau, you know I respect and love you, but I can do this. I need to see what's going on so I know whether I can treat him or if we need to call for a doctor."

He held up his hands and stood back, giving her space. Ruby had to use both hands to cut through the heavy leather of Aiden's boots. The closer she got to his feet, the more restless he became until Beau had to hold him down. She pulled the scissors away and set it to the side. Beau came to the end of the bed and peeled the boot away from the tender skin of Aiden's ankle, then off his foot.

The smell of Aiden's swollen red flesh hit Jennie's nostrils and she gagged. He had no sock left whatsoever and the inside of his boot had rubbed his foot raw. Jennie went to get a basin of water and soap while Ruby worked on the other boot.

Jack laid quietly in the kitchen and

rested his head between his paws. She knelt down and patted him on the head. "Aiden must've shown you a pretty good turn for you to change your ways so much. Thank you for helping Beau find him." She stood and tossed down the bone Ruby had pulled from the stewpot, along with a few bits of pork fat. While Jack ate his dinner, Jennie finished warming some water and brought the basin back to Beau and Ruby.

"Oh, Jennie. Thank you." Ruby wiped her brow with the back of her wrist. "It isn't good. I hope we can get this infection under control." She turned to Beau. "I need you to go get the vinegar from the kitchen."

"Aren't they pickled enough?" Beau's eyes grew wide.

Ruby ignored his attempt at humor. "It isn't for pickling. In this case, I want to clean the wound and I don't have any alcohol to do it. The vinegar should work instead."

"Or burn his foot right off his ankle..." Beau muttered under his breath as he left.

"Ruby, do you think he'll be all right?" Jennie came into the room and looked down at Aiden's pale face, her heart ached for him. If not for her, he would've ridden with them in the wagon and his feet wouldn't be as bad as they were. She winced as she looked down at

94

his ravaged feet.

"Oh yes, he just walked too far on boots that wore his feet away. I don't know how we'll replace his boots, but I suppose we'll have to. There was nothing for it, I had to cut them off."

"It's good to know. He wants to get to work so he can return to his pa. He can't do that if he can't walk." She set the basin down next to Ruby, then straightened. Her hand seemed to move of as if it had its own mind, first resting on his shoulder, then up to his still-soft cheek, lingering a little longer than she knew she should. But being in the same room with him again felt more right than she could explain. Would he wake up and tease her, or want to leave right away?

"Why don't you grab that stack of rags and bring them here." Ruby interrupted her thoughts with a gruff command. She gathered the strips of cloth and knelt next to Ruby.

Jennie whispered softly. "You can go finish in the kitchen. I'll tend to his feet. It's the least I can do. I should've known better than to jump out of the wagon with a growling dog underneath it."

"It wasn't your fault you got bit." Ruby snapped and picked up the cloths, moving them from her.

"It might not be my fault, but I should've known better. He didn't know I wasn't an animal coming to get him.

Jack was scared."

Ruby stood and washed her hands in the smaller basin by the door. "I'll be in the kitchen." She tilted her head and her eyes said she could hear everything. "Just on the other side of this wall, if you need me."

Jennie nodded and washed her hands, then carefully pulled one of Aiden's legs off the bed, dipping it into the warm water. The soft cloth soaked up the water from the basin she'd brought and she wrung it out over his ankle to wet the whole area. His foot was heavy and slippery as she gently lathered a cloth with the soap and dabbed it over the sore area, careful not to scrub. As she dipped his foot back in the water, she heard a sharp intake of breath and looked up at his beautiful hazel eyes, wide with surprise and pain.

"Didn't think I'd see you again so soon." His voice rumbled in the small space.

Jennie felt heat rush from her neck to her ears then smiled, dabbing his foot dry with a clean towel. He sat up in the bed and lifted his other leg into the water. He winced and sucked in a long breath.

"That really stings." He moaned and leaned against the wall.

Beau strode in holding a jar. He wore the look of a concerned parent as he handed it to her. "Here you go, Jennie." His hard face nodded to Aiden. "Aiden," he said before sitting in the one chair, a presiding force in the room.

Aiden rubbed his eyes and his stomach rumbled loudly. "What's in the jar?"

Beau laughed. "Jennie's going to pickle your feet so we don't have to smell them anymore."

Aiden's face turned red. "Well, if you give me my boots, I can be on my way. You don't have to put up with my *feet* no more." He shoved himself forward to sit up but wouldn't yank it from her.

Jennie washed his other foot as Aiden and Beau bantered. She tried to ignore the irritation in Aiden's voice, but it hit her deeper inside than she had any right to feel. If she could find a moment of peace to apologize, that need to speak with him would surely go away.

"You ain't going anywhere, Aiden. My wife says you have an infection in your feet and you need to sit for a couple days to let them heal. You also need some new boots because she had to cut them clean off. They wouldn't budge."

Aiden glanced from Jennie to Beau, his voice exploded around her. "You cut a man's boots off? I need those!"

Jennie carefully poured the vinegar over his feet and his body tensed as he pulled away from her. He threw his head back against the wall with a *crack*.

"I'm sorry," she whispered. "It's done

now. I just need to wrap them up."

Beau stood. "You'll have to stay here a couple days to mend. While you're here, this's your room. You'll stay on the main level of this house and won't go anywhere near the stairs, understood?"

"Yes, sir. Not like I can walk, anyway." Aiden responded bitterly as he tried to lay back on the bed. He struggled with his feet still on the floor. Jennie lifted first one, then the other for him and finished binding them. His soft, calm breathing left her sure he'd fallen back asleep and she gathered the leftover rags and basin of dirty water balanced against her waist to leave him be and let him rest. As she walked by, he reached out and grabbed her hand. She gasped and jumped at the light pressure, sloshing the water a bit.

"Jennie, I'm so sorry about what Jack did. I didn't know he'd do that, I wasn't thinking. I tied him under the wagon I was sleeping under." He grimaced. "Is your arm all right?"

She nodded, staring at his hand touching hers, trying to memorize the feeling for later when he was gone again. "Yes. Ruby said your quick action saved me from getting bitten worse. Thank you."

"I'm surprised you let my fool dog in the house after what he did to you." He pressed his thumb into her palm and her belly did a strange quiver.

"It isn't *my* home and all of us knew if Jack found us without you, something was wrong. He wouldn't have broken free of you to find us, so he had to have been looking for us to help you."

"I'm glad he was there or I'd still be in that ditch, probably until morning when, who knows what would have happened."

"You'll stay, won't you?" She closed her eyes and squeezed his hand, hoping against hope that he wouldn't run again.

"I'll stay until I can get new boots. I had a job lined up and I'm afraid I'm going to lose it."

She set the heavy basin on the table. "Tell Beau, maybe he could work in your stead, so you don't lose your place?"

Aiden shook his head and his face hardened. "It's mining. Beau already told me he wants to avoid mines. He doesn't want to get bit with the fever. Too many pretty girls to provide for." His eyes softened and smiled up at her, pressing his thumb in the palm of her hand once more. "I think I need a little rest. Thank you for bandaging me up. I'm sorry..." He turned red as a beet and glanced down to his feet.

"It's okay. It wasn't your fault. Rest now." She reluctantly released his hand

and turned down the wick on the lamp,
then left him to rest.

Chapter Eight

Aiden lay in his bed and listened to Beau and Ruby and all the girls talking. He tried to remember the last time he'd eaten and far as he could tell, it had been the noon meal two days before. A shadow darkened his doorway.

"Are you awake, Aiden?" Jennie's soft voice made him smile and the smell that came with her had his mouth watering.

"I am."

She came in balancing something in her arms, slowly making her way the few steps to the edge of his bed. She set it down, then pulled out a card of flexibles to light the lamp. It was black as pitch in the small room, but he could see Jennie in his mind's eye with little trouble.

The lamp bathed the room in soft light and her gentle features came into focus. She replaced the hurricane and smiled at him, though he was distracted by the stew sitting on the table beside him and the wonderful savory smell wafting from it.

"I heard your stomach making a fuss before and figured you could stand some supper." Jennie pulled up the chair next to his bed. "I'll stay while you eat. I already fed Jack, so don't worry. He isn't starving."

Aiden pulled himself up and sat against the wall, reached for the bowl and balanced its warmth on his chest. Jennie handed him a spoon and he took his first mouthful. Ruby sure could cook, that was fact. He closed his eyes and savored the bite.

"I talked to Beau about your job. He isn't sure what he can do about it, because he has to go find his own job tomorrow. He's hoping to find something soon."

Aiden finished his bite and swallowed. "I'm guessing I'm not in a hotel, so this must be a house. How did all of you get into a house so quick?"

"The hotel manager didn't want to deal with all of us taking all his rooms. He had this house available, but it'll be for sale. We don't know how long we'll be able to stay."

Aiden frowned. "My pack is back at that old shanty and it isn't locked. I have a little in my money belt, but I don't think I have enough for new boots. If I don't have those, I can't work in the mine."

She pulled the two dollars he'd paid for his shave from her apron and left it on the table. "Maybe you aren't supposed to. Isn't that dangerous work?" Jennie grabbed a cup of water and held it to his mouth.

She looked so worried about him. He didn't deserve anyone as pretty as her to pay him no mind. Aiden took the cup himself and drank, then handed it back to her. "Dangerous or not, it's what I know and I need to keep my promises." He ate a few more bites as he tried to think of a way to explain it to her without digging deep into his family and why he left. He'd been so young and foolish then, and he didn't want her to think of him like that. A man had to act like a man, but he hadn't then.

"What promises? I don't understand why you must do it if there're other jobs available. Why would you risk getting hurt?"

Aiden shook his head. He didn't want it to matter to her, whether he got hurt or not. "Those promises are between me and those I made them to. At some point, I have to go back and make what I did right."

Jennie's eyes pleaded with him to share with her, but he couldn't do it. He couldn't say what he knew would make her run. It was selfish to want her attention for the brief time he'd be there, but his da had always said he was selfish. This just proved again his da was right.

"Money is money, no matter where you earn it. You're hurt and you can't work in the mine for a while. Once you heal a little, why not try working somewhere else, somewhere safer?"

"Mining's all I know. You just wouldn't understand."

She clutched his arm and the warmth of her hands sent shock waves through his thin shirt all the way to his skin, and much deeper.

"So, help me understand! Why can't you at least think about doing something else?"

She will never understand and it's better to keep my promise, then return home. He pried her hand from his arm and set his jaw, then looked away from her and closed his eyes. "As soon as I can walk, boots or no, I'm going back to my home outside of town."

He heard her gasp and felt her knee nudge the bed as she stood and left. *You can find someone else, Jennie, someone who isn't beholden to a promise and a family that will never love him.*

Jennie closed the door behind her and leaned against it. She was trapped inside this big pretty house. Back in Cutter's Creek or even in Yellow Medicine, if she'd needed a minute of peace, she could leave the house and go for a walk. She couldn't do that here, it wasn't safe to go out walking alone. Though she could probably take Jack, even that wouldn't deter someone who really wanted to take her, and Ruby would never allow it.

She trudged up the stairs and flopped on her bed, no longer hungry. Her sleeve had to be repaired or she'd only have the dress she was already wearing. The bite on her arm throbbed but she ignored it. Picking up her small sewing kit, she focused on the sleeve's torn edge. Holding the needle tightly, she agonized over the stitches to make them perfect.

Hattie sauntered into their room and pulled out the chair by the small desk. She sighed loudly. "I just can't believe we're stuck here in this house with *nothing* to do. Beau made a long speech at supper about how we're to stay in the house while he's out looking for work

105

and should only leave with him. He's decided this house won't work for us since we're used to our freedom, but we must stay here until we can get a homestead. He fears we may not be able to file for a homestead without filing for a claim, but he doesn't know for sure because he hasn't checked with the land office." She rolled her eyes. "Why did we come here again?"

Jennie didn't want to argue with Hattie, didn't even want to talk to her. "We're here because it's a brand-new state, and Beau likes new places without lots of people, and Ruby would do about anything Beau said." Jennie tried to ignore Hattie and concentrate on her stitches. Over the last month, Hattie had been steadily getting under her skin, and her complaints were only making Jennie more furious.

"Well, Deadwood certainly doesn't fit that. It's bigger than where we came from!" Hattie stomped her foot.

"I don't know, Hattie. Why don't you ask him? I'm sure he thinks he's doing what's best for us and he's certainly giving it more thought than Pa ever did."

"Yeah, but at least Pa *wanted* us to get married. I don't see how we're ever going to find someone if we're forever stuck in the house."

"Reverend Level will start his preaching this Sunday, Beau and Ruby will take us over to hear him preach. Then you'll get to meet some of the townspeople."

"You have an answer for everything, don't you? Why are you so glum? Did Aiden finally tell you to skedaddle with your grumpy ways?" Hattie laughed loudly, leaning forward in her chair.

Jennie gasped and tears stung her eyes. She certainly hadn't meant to be grumpy with Aiden. He was healing. "How could you say such a thing?"

"Oh, Jennie, I didn't mean anything by it and you know it. It's just that every time you turn around, you're all sulky. You catch more flies with honey than vinegar." Hattie winked and grinned.

"Maybe I don't want to catch flies at all." She shoved the needle into the fabric and into her finger. She groaned, clutching her finger into a fist.

"You aren't fooling anyone." Hattie stood up and strode across the room, standing in front of her and narrowing her eyes. "Did you think no one noticed you dashing from Aiden's room up the stairs to avoid all of us? Don't you think we all knew exactly what happened? That you spoke your mind and you pushed him away ... again. Men aren't hard to understand, Jennie. They want what they want. You either stand with him or you stand against him. I guess you just need to figure out if Aiden is worth standing for, or if you'll step aside."

"You seem to forget that he hasn't paid you the slightest bit of attention, Hattie." Jennie glared up at her. She was not going to let her anywhere near Aiden, not when it was obvious he had no intention of sticking around anyway. He'd head out as soon as a new gold rush hit.

"Only because he's still hoping you'll settle down and pay attention. A man'll only wait so long." Hattie flounce her hip out and turned.

"What about Beau. You are two years younger than me and he hasn't given you permission to even *look* yet."

Hattie's arms stiffened at her sides and her fists clenched into quivering balls of anger. "He didn't give you permission either, Jennie. He just never held you back. If you don't want Aiden, step back, because I know a good man when I see him and if I don't get him, I'll find another way out of here. I'm ready for life, Jennie, and *this* ain't living."

"He'll be gone in two days and you'll never see him again, Hattie," Jennie screamed jumping from the bed. She wanted to throttle her sister, but she'd never listen anyway. Hattie had always been stubborn.

Hattie winced and turned her head back to Jennie. "How could you have done such a thing? He's a good man, Jennie. Don't let him go."

Jennie threw the dress down on the bed and Hattie turned to face her.

"My whole life, the only thing that's ever mattered is getting out. All Pa ever wanted was for all of us to come of age so he could get rid of us. Now I have a choice. I don't want to marry just because I can. I don't want to marry just anyone. Look at Ruby, the man Pa found for her nearly killed her!"

"Then she found Beau. Marriage doesn't have to be terrible, Jennie. In fact, it looks like it could be a lot of fun."

"Ruby picked Beau! That's completely different. I didn't pick Aiden and he didn't choose me, either. He isn't the man you think he is, Hattie. He's been bitten by gold fever and as soon as Beau knows that, he'll make him leave."

Hattie screwed up her face. "He didn't choose you? Is that what you really think? When you jumped out of the back of the wagon yesterday morning, I heard him scream and I jumped to look out the front. He was running toward our wagon with a look like I've never seen before. He was terrified. You didn't see him cradle you in his arms when he reached you, but *we* did. You might not want to admit it, but that man cares about you and you'd best consider that before you talk to him again." Hattie turned and left the room.

Jennie sat on the edge of the bed. A man shouldn't care about her, none of them. She wasn't ready for something as important as a man's heart.

Chapter Nine

Aiden let his head bump against the wall behind him, the sound keeping time with his heart. His feet throbbed their protest at the end of the bed. At least the vinegar had taken care of the smell. He'd been sure his feet were rotting and while they still hurt, they felt better. He threw back the covers and stared at them. Jennie had wrapped them in clean bandages and Ruby had come in to tell him the boots couldn't be repaired and he'd need new ones.

He shook his head, wondering what Boom must have thought when he was gone without word or even a note. Maybe Boom couldn't read, anyway. Course, if he made it to his feet, maybe he could get back to the shanty. Aiden picked up one leg and let if fall off the side of the bed. As his foot hit the floor a searing pain ran its way through his foot and up his leg and he bit back a yell. Jack poked his head in the door and tucked it low, growling at Aiden.

"It's okay, boy. It's just time for me to get out of here."

Jack growled again and Beau appeared behind him at the door. He crossed his arms over his chest and waited. Aiden scowled and lifted his other leg, letting it fall beside the other.

"So, that's how you'll handle this? You'll run? Here, if you're going to be as stubborn as a mule, let me help you." Beau strode into the room and yanked Aiden to his feet by his elbow.

Paid shot up Aiden's legs and sweat erupted all over his body. The pain burned and throbbed. Balance fled him and he wobbled, tottering beside the bed. He threw his arms out, but there wasn't anything to hold on to besides Beau, and he wouldn't give him the satisfaction of granting him help. He fell back onto the bed with a bitten off curse.

"Want to try again? Goodness knows, there's nothing more important than getting back to your *home* so you can catch a ride to the mine tomorrow morning. Never mind that we've welcomed you in since we met you. Are you a man? Are you going to let a few words from Jennie stop you? Get up. Leave."

Aiden clenched his teeth against the wave of nausea, then shook his head. "What do you know about it? Did she go running to you after I told her I was leaving?"

"She didn't have to; the walls are thin. I'm going to say what she was too smitten to say. You don't need to work in those mines to fulfil any promise. You can stay here, work hard, and go pay whoever it is you need to. Deadwood is a booming town. Miners spend money here. But, if you're going to return to mining, you leave Jennie alone. I won't have her mourning over you. She's had it tough enough."

"I am a miner, it's what I know." It even sounded hollow to his own ears and hearing that Jennie was smitten had hit him hard in the chest. He'd hoped he'd read her wrong, but if Beau had noticed, then he was right. He didn't want to carry her heart, he couldn't even be trusted with gold. "I don't want to disappoint Jennie, but the fact is, this's who I am. She can accept it, or she'll have to find someone who'll live up to what she wants. Maybe that isn't me."

Beau crossed his arms and stood back, giving him space to think. "It could be. The choice is up to you. You're welcome to stay." He turned and walked out of the room, returning a few minutes later to drop an old pair of boots by the bed.

"Jennie told me the money by the bed was for boots. They're old, but they'll do until you can buy another pair. Ruby also insisted you take this pair of socks she knitted." He tossed them on the bed. "Let us know your decision." His angry footsteps stomped down the hall, leaving Aiden alone.

He looked at the empty door then felt something cold and wet touch his hand. He patted Jack on the head without looking at him. He could make the decision to just leave, but they sure were making it hard. They wanted more from him than even his parents had, and the pressure laid heavy on him.

The dog lifted his head sharply, planting his cold wet nose against his wrist. Aiden frowned. "You want to stay, don't you, boy?"

Jack laid his head on Aiden's lap, his eyes shifting all around.

"What if I don't belong here? I might cause more trouble staying here than I started a year ago when I left home."

Jack's dark brown eyes stared up at him as a small area of drool formed on Aiden's pants.

"I can't go home until I prove I was

114

right, there's money to be made in mining."

Jack shifted and laid down at Aiden's feet. Even the dog had given up on him.

"Don't turn your back on me, Jack. It's important."

Jack lifted his head slightly and tipped his nose down. The dog was rolling his eyes.

Aiden threw up his hands. Even his dog was on Jennie's side.

Jennie heard Beau and Ruby talking in the kitchen, which was situated beneath her room. Beau hadn't yet left to look for work that morning, but would soon. Jennie wouldn't go down and disturb them; they got so few moments alone. The front door closed with a click and Jennie pushed herself up out of the bed. Hunger gnawed at her; she hadn't gone back down to eat the night before, after her argument with Hattie.

If Aiden wanted to go, she wasn't going to watch him make that choice. She'd also heard the argument between Beau and Aiden. The whole house had. Her feet dragged getting ready, unsure if Aiden left or not, and praying he hadn't made that choice on her account.

She wrapped her robe around her dress to ward off the chill in the house and padded down the stairs. Ruby waited in the kitchen, looking quite green as she stood by the pail on the dry sink.

"Ruby, what is it?" Jennie rushed over and hugged her older sister close as she quaked.

"I'm so sick, never felt so sick in my life." she sniffed. "I don't know if there's something wrong with me or the baby. Beau wants to take me to visit the doctor when he gets home."

Jennie led her over to the table and sat Ruby down, then rushed to get her some coffee. Ruby hated tea so perhaps the warmth of something familiar would help calm her stomach. She set the steaming cup in front of Ruby then ducked out of her robe and strapped on her apron. "You sit, I'll take care of breakfast. I'm so sorry, Ruby. Just rest."

Ruby rested her head against her hand and stared down into her coffee. "I'm not that far along, but we're hopeful that it's just a bug." She laid her hand on her stomach and shook her head.

"Well, don't go thinking you did anything wrong. People get sick all the time, it doesn't mean there's anything wrong." Jennie rested her hands on her hips and swallowed back her own tears. It was bad enough Ruby would have to hide her illness from the others, because they didn't know, but she shouldn't feel bad about crying in front of Jennie. "Ruby, just remember what Ma used to say, every life, under heaven, has a purpose. I don't know what's happening, or why, but I do know that He can give you hope."

"He did." A tear slid its way down Ruby's cheek.

Jennie turned, unable to blink back her tears anymore. It confounded her why the Lord might give, then take away, but the Lord had His reasons, and she'd just pray that the sickness had nothing to do with the little life growing inside Ruby. She cracked eggs into a bowl and cooked them up, dishing up portions for all her sisters, and for Aiden, in the hopes he was still there.

She looked over her shoulder at Ruby and her sisters as they slowly filed into the kitchen and sat at the table, ready to eat. She left her own plate at the table and took Aiden's into his room.

He opened his eyes as she walked in, then pushed himself up on his elbow. His hair was tousled with sleep and he was showing a bit of orange shadow around his jaw.

"It smells wonderful."

She waited for him to finish sitting up then set the plate on his lap. "I need to change your bandages. We worked hard to clean them up, wouldn't want the infection to get worse."

Aiden sighed. "Jennie, go sit with your sisters and eat. I won't go running off you." He laughed. "Probably best if you have breakfast before you deal with a man's feet, anyway. Might not want to afterward."

Something about his freshly risen appearance and his humor sparked something within her and built to a sweet glow. "Thank you, Aiden. I'll return in just a bit."

"I know *you* think I am, but I'm not a complete monster. Go. I'll still be here when you get back." He laughed and picked up his fork.

He couldn't have been more wrong about how she felt for him. Jennie took a few steps toward the door, but stopped next to his bed.

"I never said you were any such thing." She leaned down and ran the back of her fingers down his bristly cheek. She had to know what the stubble felt like against her hand. It wasn't soft anymore, yet the slight contact set her pulse racing.

Aiden reached up and captured her hand, holding it against his cheek. "You're too sweet, Jennie girl, to be wasting any of your time on me." He let go of her and fixed his focus on eating.

Her soul soared as she left the small room, though it was short-lived. As soon as she saw the pinched look on Ruby's face, she reined in her feelings.

Jennie sat down at her seat and forced a smile. "Hattie and Eva? Do you think you could work with Francis, Nora, Lula, and Daisy to get the upstairs finished today? I promised Ruby I'd work with her on a project down here and we want to keep it quiet for Aiden so he can rest."

Hattie sent her a scathing look. "I don't see why we should be stuck upstairs where it is sickeningly hot. Can't we explore the town today?"

Ruby shook her head. "No, Beau is concerned that until we know more about what's expected here, we should stay inside."

"So, we're trapped in here?" Hattie crossed her arms. "At least back home we had the freedom to move."

Daisy laid her hand on Hattie's. "It's fine. Let's make our bedrooms as nice as they can be. Maybe when Beau gets home he'll take us out to see the town."

Hattie frowned. "I wouldn't count on it. If he finds work, he'll get home late and tired." She pushed out her chair and stomped up the stairs.

Jennie interrupted. "I know that Beau and Ruby will be gone for a short while after, so he won't be able to take any of us out after supper."

Daisy folded her hands in her lap. "I'll go work on my room until it looks like what we left behind."

Ruby stood and pushed in her chair. "Thank you, Jennie and Daisy. I'm not feeling well, I'll be lying down for a bit."

Jennie watched Daisy and the others file up the stairs and when everyone was gone, she strode back to Aiden's room. He'd moved his plate off his lap and onto the small table by his bed. His head rested against the wall behind him. She took the plate out to the kitchen but returned quickly. If she could change his bandages while he slept, it might hurt him less.

She padded softly to the end of the bed and knelt by his feet. It took more patience than she realized she had to untie the bandage on each foot without moving him, but unwinding the long bandages would involve lifting his leg. She used some folded blankets and a spare pillow to raise his leg and lifted it as gently as possible. Jack whined at her feet.

"Shush, Jack. You're going to wake him up," she whispered, her hands trembling.

Aiden cleared his throat and she jumped, dropping his foot to the bed. He sucked in a deep breath as his heal dug into the cot.

"Aiden, you scared me." She backed

away from him, putting her hands behind her back. She felt like a child caught stealing.

He moved his feet around, glancing at them briefly then up at her. "They feel much better. I'm not sure what Ruby used on them yesterday, but other than being tender when they touch anything, they seem fine. Now, I just need those boots Beau found for me. He'd brought them in here last night, but they've disappeared."

"Just where do you think you're going?" She stepped forward and continued to unwind his bandages.

"I'm going home. I decided this morning, after listening to you and your sisters, that I've missed out on real riches. I haven't seen my brothers or sister in over a year. They have what makes life worth living, not anything I can find here. I just have to swallow my pride, admit I was wrong, and ask my da to take me back." He laughed humorlessly. "Should be easy, right? But, you should be happy, at least I won't be in the mines."

All the breath rushed out of Jennie's lungs and she couldn't speak for a moment as she unwrapped Aiden's other foot to avoid the hurt welling inside her. It was so foolish, he was going to go home where he belonged. Not with her. He was right, she should be happy. He wouldn't be in the mines. But for the life of her, she couldn't be. His feet looked fine, there was only so long she could use that as an excuse for her silence, she'd have to say something. The silence around her was weighted with his expectation of her answer.

"I guess if what you were looking for isn't here, then you should go," she whispered against the lump in her throat, clasping the strips of cloth tightly in her hands to hide their trembling. "I'll get those boots for you. Wouldn't want you to have to wait around here too long." Her voice lodged in her throat.

She tried to flee the room but Aiden reached out and grasped her hand. Drat the cramped room that allowed him to reach her! "Jennie, what's the matter? You're never this quiet. I thought you'd be happy. I'm not going back to the mines. It's what you wanted."

She wouldn't look down at him. "I'm sorry. I have a lot of work to do. This is a big house." She pulled free of him, a little more forcefully than was necessary, and left the room as a tear escaped down her cheek. When Beau had found Aiden again, she'd thought he would be around long enough to convince him he didn't need to work in the mines. Now that he'd decided against mining, he would leave her behind. Stuck in Deadwood.

Chapter Ten

Aiden lifted his feet one at a time and flexed his toes. They weren't painful or achy now, he just had to get his boots. Jennie hadn't come to see him in the two days since he'd told her he was going home. Since then, no matter who came in to feed him, they didn't bring them and he couldn't leave the room without them. While he wasn't a man of great manners, walking around the house barefoot wasn't an option unless you were a toddler. Jennie's distance, and the fact that she hadn't brought the boots like she'd said, bothered him. Her distance had forced him to think about her, far more than was good for him.

He gingerly put one foot than the

other on the floor and tested his weight on them. Finding them as good as ever, he stretched up on his toes then back down. Standing felt wonderful after lying in bed for days. He found the socks Beau had left with him near the ointment at the end of his bed. He slipped them on and relished the warm comfort of new wool socks. He walked to the door of his little room and Jack yipped at him.

Aiden patted the dog's head and moved further out into the short hall that led to the kitchen. Ruby stood by the stove stirring something in a large pot.

She glanced up and a smile played at her lips. "Aiden, so good to see you up and walking about. I was resting a bit the last few days myself and took that time to knit you some more socks. I'll get them for you."

She tapped her spoon on the side of the pot and rushed to the stairs, returning a minute later with another pair of black socks. He held them for a moment, feeling their thickness. He hadn't had a new pair of socks in longer than he could remember and now he had two.

"Thank you, Ruby. I won't forget your kindness." He sat at the table and she set a cup of coffee in front of him. He felt better now that he was up and moving.

Beau came in and kissed Ruby on the back of the neck. "Aiden, I have those boots near the door." He dug around and pulled out the old pair of boots he'd brought before. Beau dropped them by his feet and waited as Aiden tried them on. They fit as well as any other boots he'd ever had before, which wasn't great, but expected.

Ruby turned and smiled. "Jennie tells us you plan to head out soon. Heading home. That's wonderful."

"Yes, ma'am. I'll need to work to earn a railroad ticket. But then I'm going home to my family."

"That's good to hear. But you'll have to keep in touch. You feel like family now." She turned back to the stove.

The words struck him. It was true. Beau and Ruby felt like family and he would miss them. The younger Arnsby girls had all wound their way into his heart like little nieces. Jennie, though, as hard as he tried, he couldn't picture her in the same way.

Beau sat at the table across from him. "They need a type-setter at the paper where I work. It'd be easier for you if you can read."

"I can." He stood and tested the boots, flexing his toes within them, glad there were no rough spots to poke holes in his new socks.

"Then you can come with me tomorrow morning. It's messy work, but nothing like the mine. If you can carve, they may even have you making the blocks, that would earn you more money, quicker."

"I don't aim to make this a profession. I just need to work long enough to earn my way south."

"It shouldn't take too long, maybe a month or so. You're welcome to stay here as long as you need. You know that."

He tried to keep his emotions in check. A month was a long time. Too long. If he let himself think about Jennie for a month, he'd be too attached. Either way, he had to find out what a ticket cost and see if his pack with the little money he had left was still where he'd left it. "I'd like to go back to the cabin Boom gave me before I ended up here. I left my bag back there."

"I'd take Jack with you. I've heard there are two places you want to avoid in Deadwood, the shanty town and Chinatown, whether either warning is true, I don't know, but that's what people tell me."

"I'll keep that in mind." He whistled for Jack and headed for the door. "Thank you, Beau, Ruby." He plopped his hat on his head and tipped it to her.

Beau smiled. "Don't thank me yet. You haven't put in a day of work."

126

KARI TRUMBO

Aiden let Jack run around the front of the house as he closed the door. The fresh summer air buzzed with expectation. He'd been chained to that room because of his feet for too many days. The sun was high in the sky and he realized Beau must have come home during the midday meal. He'd lost all track of time. Even with the small window in his room, the light never seemed to fully make it into the space. Tilting his face back, he closed his eyes and let the sun warm his face. The weather was so much different than Kansas or California. It was like the best of both.

He made his way down the streets, following the glimpses of the shanty town he could see as he went by rows of homes. The closer he got, the older and more decrepit the houses appeared. He walked by a few homes that were little more than burned out shells. Blackened boards stuck out at odd angles from deep craters. Some houses were still upright, but gray with soot, the glass in the windows long gone, and tattered curtains fluttering in the breeze. He shook his head. That was the mark of enough devastation to make a man pick up his family and leave...if the families who'd lived in those homes even survived.

As he walked down the rows of tiny homes in the shanty town not a soul was in sight. Every working man was off in the mines. There wasn't a woman or child, not dog or even chickens, to be seen. Even the cribs were quiet. He searched for and finally found his small place. The door remained open, hanging precariously off the makeshift hinges as it had when he'd gotten there.

He pushed the door further open and saw the tick he'd spent the day filling was now flat and clothes he didn't recognize hung on the pegs on the wall. Boom had already given away his home to someone else, so where was his saddle? He searched through the few things inside, but his saddle was gone, probably sold.

A coldness lay on him as he closed the door behind him to leave. His da had got him that shaving kit when he'd finally started taking on whiskers. The pack and saddle itself had been a gift from his older brother. He'd carried it for more miles than he could count because it was all he'd had left of his family and he couldn't leave it behind. Now, his travels away from home had cost him everything. His snide insistence that the world held something better than what he'd had rang hollow in his ears. How would they ever forgive him?

He trudged back to Deadwood with Jack on his heels. His shoulders slumped and he passed Beau's house as he walked further up town. There were

128

shops, barbers, grocers, restaurants, and other businesses that he only noted in passing. What he needed was the railroad station. Deadwood's rail system wasn't old, but it'd been carrying mining equipment for a few years. It had only recently connected with three other nearby rail systems to take passengers to and from Deadwood, making it more appealing and accessible. Though his only interest was in how to leave, and if those few rail systems connected with a major one to get him home. He searched the fare board and found what he was looking for. The new lines didn't go many places; he'd have to connect at another larger station further south.

It would cost him thirty dollars to get home. If he could get the pay Boom had told him about as a miner, he could leave within two weeks. If not, he'd be here longer. There was just no way to know what Beau's job would offer until he showed up to check it out. Thirty dollars was a daunting amount when he currently made nothing. And four weeks was a lifetime when he had to leave quickly or risk caring too much. If he cared too much, he might not ever go home and make things right.

The walk back to the large house was a short one. His feet had already begun to throb and the front steps would make an excellent place to rest out of the way of the ladies in the house. While mining might not have been good for him, his body was in good condition because of it; swinging a pick for a year on the prospector's claim had worked fine for him. He'd been younger, and foolish to think the old man would give him his share. But here...miners were under contract and the experienced ones could make as much as seven dollars a day. He was sorely tempted to find Boom. But there was always the possibility Boom would be no different than the old coot in California.

He let himself fall comfortably on the steps of the porch back at the Rockford's and let the sun shine on him. Jack sat next to him and rested his head on Aiden's leg. He stroked the dog's ears but let his mind wander. During the day, the city of Deadwood was an amazing ruse. It looked much like any bustling western town. They lived on the edge of the municipality where a few stores were still wooden with high false fronts painted white with bold black lettering announcing their business to the world. Men in white aprons, sleeves rolled high, helped farmers bring cattle in to the back for butchering. He'd walked by just about any business a man could imagine.

The door clicked behind him and he heard the rustle of petticoats swish toward him. It was strange how Jennie could use the very same soap as the rest of her family, but he could tell without turning that the scent of rose soap clung to *her*. He turned and she joined him, sitting a few feet away on the other end of the step. Her hair was the same color as a flake of gold and it shone just the same in the sunlight. She laid her hands in her lap and searched the area around them. Jack got up and went to her, plopping down by her side and licking her face. She laughed and patted her lap. Jack immediately obeyed and laid his head down for some attention. That dog was stealing his girl.

"How's your arm?" he mumbled, at a loss for what else to say.

She stopped petting Jack and touched her forearm. "Fine, it wasn't as bad as it looked at first. He's so good now, it's hard to imagine he did that."

"I think he was just scared. He'd been rescued the night before; the camp was new with different noises... I'm so sorry, Jennie."

She turned her face away and brushed a strand of hair behind her ear. "You already apologized and I forgave you. It wasn't your fault. When do you think you'll go?" Her face didn't change but her body did, and Jack noticed the change as much as he did, whining at the sudden tension in her shoulders and back.

"Well, that all depends on that job

Beau has for me. If I can make what I would've in the mine, less than two weeks. If not..." he shrugged, he couldn't lie to her about his desire to go quickly. She would take it wrong and part of him still wanted to stay with the golden-haired beauty next to him, even if it was dangerous.

She turned toward him. "And will you go work in the mine if you can't get that much with Beau?" Her face was set, just as it had been when he first joined them. She'd already shut him out and counted him as gone.

"No, that isn't my plan. I'm not strong enough to say no. If I started in the mine, it would be too easy to think *just one more day and I'll be richer, just one more day until I strike it big.* I may go home with nothing in my pockets for my da except an apology. I've got to pray that's enough."

She nodded. "So, what you really want *is* in Deadwood, you're just not willing to let yourself go for it. Temptation is a terrible thing."

He clenched his hands to keep from reaching out to her. No one knew about the difficulty of temptation more than him at that moment. He glanced away from her. "The cost of searching for gold is much higher than buying it. I see that now. Is Ruby going to be all right?" He ran his hand up the back of Jacks fur and scratched his neck, using the dog as an excuse to inch closer to Jennie.

Jennie hid a smile as she tucked her chin. "Yes, the doctor says it's pretty common to get sick. We didn't know. Mama never got sick with us."

"What do you mean?"

Jennie cocked her head to the side and smiled faintly. "I guess I can tell you, since she finally told the family. Ruby is in a family way."

For some reason her words came back to him and he wished he could've been included in the celebration. She must have told them when he was out of the house or he'd have heard it.

Jack rolled off Jennie's leg and turned over between them. His lips flopped open like a lopsided grin. Jennie laughed and her face softened.

"I've never seen a dog do that before." He couldn't take his eyes off Jennie, and he said a prayer she didn't notice. "I wish I knew where he came from. I guess he's mine now, though I don't know if they'll let him travel by train."

"Maybe you'll just have to leave him here... with me." She glanced up at him, her eyes asking for much more than the dog.

He wanted to give her assurances, but he couldn't. If da didn't forgive him, he'd work hard until he could earn forgiveness. Jennie was too good a girl to make wait. He'd never considered coming back, though, maybe it was possible. He still couldn't give her hope where there might be none. "I can't do that. Might be tempted to come back and get him. Like you said. Temptation is a terrible thing." He stood up and strode into the house before Jennie could make him admit more than he wanted to. Talking with that girl always made him feel as if more was being said than he meant, and he hated the tight feeling in his chest whenever he thought about what to say. He hated it even more when he left her.

Jennie bustled around Ruby in the kitchen, keeping busy. Nothing seemed to relieve the knot in her stomach. Aiden had said he'd be gone within two weeks, after that she could relax again. Every time she got near him and worse, if she opened her mouth, her stomach would get to fluttering and her heart would speed up. Then her hands felt clammy and she had to mentally stop herself from wiping them on her skirt. She worried about her hair being just right or if her dress was just so. She tugged on her bodice, the pins she'd placed earlier to hold the dress so it would fit poked into her skin.

Jennie shook away the tense feeling in her hands and opened the oven to check the bread. Aiden would be joining them at the table that night and she'd already known she couldn't eat in front of him, especially if her stomach wouldn't cooperate. The bread was done and she grabbed the metal handle that would click into the groove on the bread pan so she could pull it out. Once it was out, she set it up on the cooling rack to finish.

Ruby and Jennie had been working in the kitchen for a few hours when the door opened, Jack barked, and Beau came in.

"Hello, lovely ladies." He swept Ruby into his arms and kissed her soundly. Jennie turned away as the heat crept up her cheeks. Her parents had never shown such displays and it made her nervous. It seemed inappropriate to look, yet they were right there in the middle of the room.

"You're home a little early." Ruby glanced out the window. The sun was still high in the sky.

"Mr. Carmichael was glad to hear we would have another worker, at least temporarily, and he sent me home a little early today. With Aiden there to help, I might be home at this time every day for the next few weeks."

"Well, good. I'm glad of it. Get washed up then sit down. We can be finished by the time you're done." She turned back to Jennie. "Why don't you go let Aiden know it's supper time?"

Jennie wiped her hands on a towel and lifted her apron over her head, then hung it on the wall. She felt the knot inside her coil tighter as she strode to his room. She knocked and the knot tightened further, making it difficult to breathe.

"It's open," he called from inside.

Jennie pushed the door open and stood in the doorway. The room was lit with a candle and Aiden sat at his small table reading.

"It's time to eat, best get washed up." She backed out of the doorway.

"Jennie, come in and look at this." He motioned her into the room.

She hesitated and her chest felt as if it would collapse under the pressure. She strode forward, forcing herself to put one foot in front of the other until she was beside him.

He pointed to a photograph of Deadwood from a few years before. "I found this in the desk. Probably a gift to the maid or whoever stayed in this room. It was used like a diary, and they kept track of all the news, the railroad coming, Crazy Horse, Wild Bill Hickock, and the building of the Grand Central Hotel—it's all here." He looked up at her with the wonder of a child at Christmas.

"I keep praying Deadwood has moved beyond all that but you want to *keep* that history?" She took a step back, unable to think clearly with him so near.

He closed the book and his expression fell. "You have to understand the history of a place to appreciate it, Jennie. A place is like a person; it has a past that makes it what it is. Deadwood had a rough beginning and it won't be tamed quickly. This is a mining town and it probably always will be. That Homestead mine will keep America in gold for a long time, mark my words. And where there's gold, there's miners. That's just a fact of life."

"Why are you so interested in the history here if you're leaving?" She rested her hand on the back of his chair as her legs urged her to run.

"Because it's interesting. This book was written by someone who loved Deadwood and was proud to see the growth. There were things they didn't like, the caravan of prostitutes for instance, including Madam Dirty Em, for one."

Jennie felt heat rise up her collar. She wasn't ignorant of what went on between husband and wife, or what happened in brothels, but it wasn't usually brought up in conversation.

"I'm so glad. You can take that book with you when you go home. It'll help you remember us and maybe you can pray for us and ask the Lord to help Deadwood." She turned to leave the room, but he took her hand and heat shot up her arm, enflaming her face, trailing warmth all the way to her heart.

"I'll pray that, at some point, you'll see the beauty of the place you live, even if you don't appreciate every last thing about it. I'll be out in just a few minutes." He regarded her hand in his and stroked the side with his thumb, sending shivers through her. The tension inside her squeezed until she was sure she couldn't take another moment. He pulled her hand closer, glanced up at her, catching her gaze. He drew her hand closer still, until she was sure he'd kiss it. She held her breath and couldn't look away if she tried. He sighed and closed his eyes then let it go and turned away.

She was left with warmth rising in her and nothing she could do would quench it. How could she teach her body that wanting a man would lead to hurt? She wouldn't let anyone force her to marry. Beau and Ruby had even promised. But she didn't want to get married at all, especially with a man whose vice could be as bad as her own Pa's had been. Not for the first time, she wished

her mother were there to tell her what
to do.

Chapter Eleven

Aiden woke early and joined Beau at the table for breakfast before they'd head down to the newspaper for work. He finished off his eggs and set his fork aside. "You don't strike me as a newspaper man, Beau." He'd yet to form a friendship with the man. They'd shared too many heated words for that. But it would have to change if they were to work together.

Beau glanced up and finished chewing. "I'm not. I've never done this before. I've always worked with horses or cattle in the past, or the railroad for a time, but there's too many people there. A man can't think."

"Well, if that isn't what you want to do, why are you doing it?" He leaned back and waited.

"Why? I don't know if you noticed, but I have a lot of mouths to feed and I can't provide for them if I'm not in town. It might be what I love, but I love those girls more. Fact is, cowboy work don't pay any better than what I'm doing now but, the jobs just aren't here. So, working for the paper was a good substitute."

Aiden could well understand the draw. It was something to keep in mind for himself. If he ever took a bride, he'd have to think about her, and maybe later the *leanbh* she'd have. "But don't you miss it? Don't you wake up every day and wish you could go do what you want?"

"Of course. This is only temporary. When I can secure a position that will provide a place for them, I can consider going back to it. But they can't live in a bunkhouse. So, for now, I don't want to be gone for days at a time."

Aiden laughed. "You ain't been married that long, then, huh?"

"Only since the day after New Year's, so, a little over five months. We've had the girls with us since the day after we were married, but until we left for Deadwood, they stayed with their mother at a different house."

A jolt of shock ran through him. "Their mother? I just assumed she was dead since she wasn't here."

"Naw, Maeve is back in Cutter's

Creek. She and a man named Carlton Williams, where the girls were staying, seemed to have come to some kind of agreement."

"So, will they want to go back and join her?" An uneasiness fell over him, thinking Jennie wouldn't remain where he left her. Even if he wasn't nearby, he liked knowing right where he could find her.

"There was some talk of it, but we won't go anywhere until the railroad has more options. I'm not making that trip by wagon, again."

Aiden nodded and drank the last of his coffee. "I don't blame you, that wasn't an easy trek."

"We'd best get a move on. Don't want you to be late on your first day."

"Do you have any idea what he might be paying? I've got to pull together thirty for my trip."

"I can't guarantee you anything, but I can tell you that I get a dollar a day."

"A dollar! It'll take me three times as long working for the paper as it would if I went to work at the mine for the least they pay experienced miners!" His fist clenched and he held back from slamming it into the table. He'd never be able to leave in two weeks, not at that pay.

"There's no guarantee you'd get that pay. You may know your way around a mine in California, but that don't mean anything here. There's a pecking order and you're at the bottom. You'd have to work your way up just like everyone else, and at the paper that starts at a dollar a day."

Aiden wanted to argue. A year's worth of picking should account for something, but the fact was he couldn't prove it. While he could probably easily work through the ranks, he didn't want to be there that long. If he had to make a dollar a day anyway, it might as well be at a job where he could come home at night.

Both men stood and Aiden put his plate next to Beau's, then grabbed his hat and the lunch pail Ruby had left for him. So, he'd have to stay a month for sure, at least he'd make it home to Kansas by harvest. Would his da even allow him back after all he'd said and done? He was a disgrace, an embarrassment.

Beau strode through the door and Aiden followed for the short walk to the newspaper office. Mr. Carmichael stood behind a high counter, waiting for them. His hands were covered in ink and he wore a white smock over his clothes.

"Ah, you must be Aiden Bradly. Beau told me you're looking for some temporary work. Well, we've got the work. Temporary or no. The miners might have started this town, but some of us are here for more than the gold. I'd like to see this town prosper and the *Deadwood*

Times is the best way to highlight the areas we'd like to enrich."

Aiden nodded. He couldn't agree more, though setting letters into the molds didn't seem like much work. Mr. Carmichael led him back to the press.

"This is where you'll do most of your work. The press needs to be maintained to run properly. It must be cleaned between uses, and the plates need to be made before each run. All those jobs will fall to you and Beau. Can you handle it?"

He nodded. "Yes, sir."

Mr. Carmichael left and Beau grabbed a rag and cleaning solution. "They did a print run yesterday, so today, we clean the machine."

Aiden grabbed a rag and took a deep breath. This work would have to do until he made enough to go home. He scrubbed the machine as he calculated the days remaining in his time in Deadwood.

Jennie took to knitting as soon as her morning chores were done. Beau had argued against them visiting around the town yet, so they stayed indoors and did chores or other tasks that had left her fingers itching for something to do. Beau had brought home a few bolts of fabric and some of the others were sewing to keep busy.

Jennie counted her stitches and started on the heel. She didn't understand why she wanted to be around Aiden but also wanted to avoid him at the same time. He'd leave in a month and she could only hope everything would calm down then, but what if it didn't? What if the feeling of expectancy, the need to be with him, only got worse after he left? What would she do then? It certainly wasn't possible to go with him.

Jack lay at her feet and nudged her toe with his nose. She knew he needed to go outside, and since the others were busy, she knew it was up to her to let him out.

"Come on, boy." She took Jack to the back door and opened it. An old man stood by the fence between both houses.

"Ho, there! Who are you? I don't recognize you. How many girls you got in that house, anyway?" His voice cracked.

Jennie stepped outside and glanced at Jack, then took a few steps toward the man. "I'm Jennie and we've lived here for a little over a week, but we tend to stay inside." Something told her he wasn't safe to talk to and shouldn't know just how many of them there were.

"Hmm, and how many of you are there?" He scratched his chin.

"Well, it doesn't really matter. Beau and Aiden make sure we're well taken care of."

"Beau and Aiden? What, do they keep an eye on you?"

She bit her lip and checked to see if Jack was finished. "I suppose, they're working right now."

"That's interesting. A fella could get used to having such pretty neighbors." He touched his hat and walked back to his house.

Though she wore long sleeves, Jennie could feel the prickling of the hair on her arms and she rubbed them as she called to Jack. Something about that old man made her uneasy. Jack bumped her leg as he ran back into the house and Jennie followed.

She closed the door and barred it, letting her unease lift as the heavy plank fell into place. As she strode through the house, someone knocked on the front door and Ruby stood from her mending to answer it. Jack growled and barked. Ruby swung the wood slat for the peep hole and stood on her toes.

"I don't recognize him." She turned back to Jennie. "Beau said not to open the door for anyone but him, the owner of the house, or Reverend Level."

146

Jack growled again and sat in front of the door.

Jennie shook her head. "We shouldn't open that door with Jack acting that way."

Ruby nodded. "You're right." She opened the peep hole once again and yelled, "I'm sorry. Please come back later when Mr. Rockford is home. Thank you!"

Jennie couldn't hear what the man said in reply, but Ruby turned quite red and swung the peep hole closed quickly.

"What an incredibly rude man." She shook her head and stepped far away from the door as if she could dodge the words the man had said. "I'll be all the happier when we get out of town. Beau has a lead for work on a cattle ranch. He never expected that to be an option out here, he tells me ranching is fairly new to this area and they're looking for experienced men."

"So, where does that leave Aiden?" Jennie asked, hoping Ruby wouldn't dig too deeply into why she'd want to know.

"Well, if he can learn quickly, it'll be a good job for him. If he wants it."

Jennie wondered what it would be like to live on a ranch, free to roam again, but Beau and Aiden had both just started. If they left, it might mean trouble for the paper. "That's true. What will the newspaper man do?"

Ruby shrugged her indifference. "I'm

sure he'll do whatever he did before we pulled into town. Beau thinks it'll be safer for all of you out on a ranch where you can leave the house, do some chores, have life pretty much like you did in Cutter's Creek."

"It'd be nice. Hattie will be happy because a ranch means cowboys." Jennie laughed.

Ruby joined her. "That's true. I don't think Hattie will complain one bit. She even asked me if I could make her dresses a little tighter and more to the fashion. She wants to show off a bit."

"That reminds me. When I'm done knitting socks for Aiden, I should take these two dresses of mine and finally tailor them to fit me properly. The pins are bothersome. I didn't do it on the way here because the wagon was bouncy, but now that we're here and can't leave, it seems like I should take the time to do it."

Ruby smiled and patted her arm. "I think Aiden would love to see you in a dress that actually fits." Ruby pinched the arm of Jennie's dress and pulled it out about three inches. "Puffy sleeves might be in style, but only if they're made that way, not because the gown was made for someone much larger than you."

Jennie tugged away. She'd only pinned the dress at the waist, but now she could see the rest of the dress looked silly. "We knew finding dresses for all of us would be difficult. I'm just glad I have them."

The doorknob wiggled and Ruby ran back to check. She smiled brightly and threw open the lock, letting Beau and Aiden in.

Beau took off his hat as he walked in the door. "I love coming home for a meal even if I'm still eating from a bucket." He swung the pail that Ruby had packed for him that morning. "Mind if we eat here?"

"Not at all! We just had the strangest visitor. I think he thought this was a women's boarding house." Ruby flushed red again.

Jennie pulled out two glasses from the cupboards then pumped water for Beau and Aiden. It was a good excuse to stay in the kitchen and sit across from Aiden. "How was your first morning?"

He glanced across the table at her and gave a half smile. "It's work, that's for sure. I'll be making quite a bit less than I would've in the mine, so I'll be here a month or so. What do you think of that, Jennie-girl?" He reached across the narrow table and gently tugged on her ear.

She shook her head as her face flushed at his attention. "It isn't up to me at all. You do what you need to do and we'll be here."

149

She stood and turned away to stop the fluttering in her belly. She could handle two weeks of the mounting tension, but a whole month... Just sitting with him made her want to drum her fingers on the table. She had too much energy and nowhere to let it out.

"How are your feet?" She began washing the counters without paying any attention to them.

"My feet are just fine. You and Ruby did a good job with them, thank you."

Beau set down his sandwich. "I'm waiting to hear back from Ferguson about the foreman position at that ranch. That would pay much better than the newspaper."

Aiden finished his bite. "Do they have room for me, too?"

Beau sat back and regarded Aiden. "I think you're old enough to pick what you want for yourself. If I get the job, he already told me he needed a couple extra hands. You'd be welcome, since I know you can ride. If I had to guess, pay would be about the same. If you stay here, expenses would be the difference, you'd have to rent somewhere and pay for your meals. If you take a job out there, your room and board would be covered like it is now."

"That's a big draw, since I want to save every cent." Aiden rested hands covered in black ink on the table. He'd washed, but the ink wouldn't budge. She glanced up to his eyes to find him staring at her, she turned and went back to her counter, the tension in her belly twisted tighter.

"The choice is yours, but you don't have to worry yet because I haven't heard from Ferguson."

Aiden nodded and downed the rest of his water. "We'd best get back to it."

Beau finished his bite and washed it down. "Yup. Thank you, Ruby, for letting us mess up your table."

She stood and kissed him on the temple. "You can dirty my table whenever you like."

Jennie wiped the crumbs while Ruby saw the men out.

After they'd left, Ruby returned and crossed her arms over her chest. "I'm tired of being cooped up in here like a nesting hen. I wanted to come here for the wide-open spaces and I haven't seen a single thing besides the doctor's office."

A sweat broke out on Jennie's forehead and her stomach turned from tight to sour. "But, Ruby, I don't think it's a good idea to go out. Beau will find us a place with peace and quiet and *then* we can all enjoy the out of doors again."

"I just want to go to the store, buy some flour and salt, and come right home. I think there's a mercantile just a few blocks down from here. If I can't walk a few blocks, we have no business in this town. If you'd rather stay here, then do so. I'll take Jack."

Jennie stood in indecision. It would be good to get out of the house, but if anything happened to Ruby, the others would be left alone until Beau and Aiden returned. Ruby reappeared with her hat in her hand.

"Well? What do you say? Are you coming or staying?"

Jennie glanced down at her feet, the overwhelming cloud over her pressed down hard. "Why don't you take Hattie with you? Two are better than one, but I'd best stay here with the younger ones."

"Wise plan. In case anything should go wrong, not that I expect it to, you'll be here." She called up the stairs for Hattie and turned back to Jennie. "Do take a few minutes this afternoon and work on your dresses. It would be worthwhile. You'll just have to trust me on that."

Jennie refused to think too long on Ruby's words. She and Beau spoke in whispers every night, but she didn't take to listening to them. She sighed as Ruby and Hattie left, clicking the lock into place. The heaviness in her chest nearly crushed her as she prayed they would return safely.

Chapter Twelve

Aiden followed Beau into the house, wiping his feet by the door as Jennie ran into the room. Her eyes were wide with tear streaks down her face, and all the air in his lungs slammed into his chest at the sight of the fear in her eyes.

"Don't take off your boots! Ruby left just after lunch with Hattie to go to the market and hasn't returned."

Beau turned back to the door and shoved Aiden out of the way as he rushed out.

Aiden searched Jennie's face. Her forehead was lined with worry and she clasped her hands in front of her.

"Oh, Aiden. What if..."

"Shh." He pulled her into his arms

and held her close, willing her to stop trembling. She fit just perfectly in his arms and her shaking seemed to dissolve as he held her close. "I've got to go help Beau. He'll need me. Don't hold supper, feed the others." He allowed himself to brush his lips over the top of her head, then he pulled himself away and followed Beau.

"I'll wait up. Please find them!" she called after him.

He dashed outside, smiling when he heard her lock the door behind him. Aiden ran and caught up to Beau a few blocks ahead of him.

Beau slammed his fist into his hand. "Why would she leave, Aiden? I told her to stay put. I just don't understand how the house could get under her skin so quickly."

"Well, didn't you say you used to take odd jobs just to get out of town? Maybe she's cut from the same cloth? How long could *you* stay pent up in the house?"

Beau shook his head. "I should've made time to go shopping with her. I don't know what I'll do if I don't find her."

"We'll find her. Jennie said she went to the mercantile. Where is it?" He stopped and glanced up and down the street.

"It's a little further down, but there's

no chance she'd still be there. It's been hours since lunch."

"I think we should go see if she made it there at all." Aiden pushed him further along the street but kept his eyes open for any sign of bright red hair. That hair might be worth a fortune to a madam. Beau pushed his way through a clutch of men by the front door and strode up to the front counter.

"Excuse me, I'm looking for someone who may have come in here earlier. She's about six inches shorter than me, dark red hair, with a younger blond about the age of sixteen."

The shopkeeper scratched his chin. "An old man came in after they paid for their purchases to help them home. Don't know where they went to after that."

"An old man... was he in a preacher's collar?" Aiden rested his hands on the counter to keep from clenching them.

The shopkeeper laughed. "No, he surely wasn't."

"Come on, Beau. Let's ask around in the street. Someone was bound to notice something." He pulled Beau's arm and could feel the tension. Beau didn't look outwardly scared, but Aiden could tell he was in knots. *He* would be.

Beau wiped the side of his mouth with the back of his hand and followed Aiden out of the mercantile. "Ruby wouldn't have accepted help from just anyone. She isn't that trusting. Hattie tends to want to attract attention and that's what scares me. Hattie may have put them both in danger."

"I think Hattie has too long been a child in the middle of a big family. She wants people to notice her away from her sisters." Aiden looked up and down the street and dodged between passing wagons, leading Beau through town. "I guess I should've paid more attention to her when she was looking for it, but I didn't want to give her the wrong idea."

Beau's bottom lip disappeared as his mouth flatlined. "I don't need anyone giving attention to Hattie just yet. Not for any reason."

Aiden stood as tall as he could and noticed a squat building on the other side of the street. It gave him an idea.

"Where're you off to?" Beau asked, his voice high.

"The stage coach station. If Ruby and Hattie were taken, the scoundrels wouldn't keep them here in Deadwood, or we'd find them right away. I'm going to check and see if any women left on the stage this afternoon."

Beau yelled over the din. "Pray they didn't. Those stages make a lot of stops and if the girls were taken, they could force them off anywhere and we'd never find them."

A sick feeling left Aiden trembling all

the way down to his boots. If they ended up down in one of the cribs in the shantytown... No, he wouldn't even give that thought credence. A few men hung around the front of the station. It was a low, one-story log building, with a plank roof. It looked like it had been thrown up in a pinch and then was just left to run as it was. Aiden rushed through the door into the dark interior. A man with a corncob pipe sat on a stool behind a counter reading a newspaper. He glanced up at them and set down his reading.

"What can I do for you? Stage won't leave again until morning."

Beau pushed forward next to Aidan and spoke first. "I'm looking for two young women. A redhead and a blond that may have been taken by stage out of town."

"Been taken? I don't know what kind of establishment you think I run here mister, but I don't like what you're suggesting."

Aiden cleared his throat. "Two ladies are missing, we're looking for them, that's all he's saying, sir." He shot a warning glance at Beau. Riling up the locals would only make the job more difficult.

"A young blond lit out on the three o'clock stage to Lead. She was leaning and pawing all over the man she was with, though. Don't sound like she was *taken* anywhere."

Beau shook his head. "That wouldn't be our girl. She may want attention, but not that badly, and she'd be with Ruby."

Aiden nodded and touched his hat. "That doesn't sound like our blond. Thank you for your time."

Beau and Aiden left the dark building and continued their search. "Let's go talk to the reverend, then the hotel owner, they are the only two people we know in town. Maybe they heard something."

Aiden scoured the street for familiar faces as he kept up with Beau. He pushed his way into the hotel and rang the bell at the front desk. An older man came out from a small door behind the counter.

"Beau, can I help you?" He pulled on the garter around his arm and shifted his gaze from one man to the other.

"I hope so, Lance. When I came home today, two of my girls were missing. They went to the mercantile and never returned. Has anyone said anything to you or have you seen them?"

Lance scratched his head. "I haven't heard anything, Beau. I'm sorry. I'll keep an ear out. I hope you find them."

Aiden cocked his head to the side and frowned. "I don't suppose you've seen Ferguson around?"

Beau glared at Aiden. "What does

that have to do with anything?"

Lance scratched behind his neck and gave a noncommittal shrug. "I saw him this morning. Not sure why it matters."

Aiden rested his hands on his waist, the man's eyes were too shifty, as if he were hiding something and this wasn't the time to let something like that slide by. "It matters because if Ferguson mentioned he was thinking about hiring Beau, it would mean you would lose the rent on that big old house."

Lance's eyes flashed and he slammed his hands down on the front desk. "Hogwash. I'll be selling that house soon. I wouldn't do anything to anyone." He crossed his arms over his chest and glared at them.

"Come on, Aiden. Let's go check with the reverend." Beau pulled Aiden's arm as he left the hotel. "We aren't going to get anywhere with Lance. If we don't find anything else, we can always go back to check the hotel again. But... I've got this terrible feeling she isn't here anymore." Beau trudged to a small house on the edge of town.

"I didn't even know where the Reverend lived." Aiden looked around at the small houses shoved together without an inch of space between them, yet clean, with tidy painted fronts in a row.

"I wouldn't say he lives here..." Beau turned back to him. "He stays here while he preaches. I'm not even sure if he's still here or if he's moved on." He strode forward and knocked on the door of one of the homes.

A little old woman answered. "What can I do for you, sir?" her voice waivered and she stared up at him.

"Is Level still here, or has he moved on, ma'am?"

She stepped to the side and opened the door further. Beau stepped inside and Aiden followed. Reverend Level sat on a chair next to the couch. Someone lay on the couch, red hair peeking from beneath a blanket.

Beau rushed to the couch and knelt in front of his wife. He brushed the hair back from her face to reveal a dark knot on the side of her head.

Level cleared his throat. "Just who I was hoping to see. A friend brought Ruby to me earlier. She was screaming in the street and someone hit her over the head. My friend took exception to anyone treating a lady like that and removed her from the situation. Ruby has quite a lump on her head, but we've been caring for her as best we know how."

"I can't tell you how glad I am that you have her. Did your friend mention any other women? Her sister Hattie was with her." Beau pulled the blanket down and touched her hands and shoulders gently, checking for injuries. Aiden stepped forward and winced, her temple was a vicious purple.

"He didn't mention anyone with her. Just that she was screaming which drew his attention, then he saw her get hit. I don't know what transpired that he ended up with her. I didn't ask for specifics."

Beau laid his head against Ruby's. "We'll never find her. She could be anywhere."

Level stood and patted Beau on the shoulder. "I will pray for her and so should all of you. I didn't know Hattie was missing, or I would've asked more questions, but I can seek out information tomorrow. Perhaps I'll find out more."

"Thank you, Reverend. I'll get her home and let her sisters take care of her, if you think she'll be okay to move."

"You'll draw attention to her without a cart. You may use mine. Allow me to hitch up my horse."

Beau nodded. "Thank you, sir."

The old woman approached him and gave Beau a cloth. "For her bump." She touched her own head.

He brushed Ruby's red hair away from her face and laid the cloth over the large bump. Beau cradled her head in his hands and kissed her forehead and cheeks, mumbling something Aiden couldn't hear. Until a few days ago, if

161

he'd seen that, he would've called the man a fool, weak. Now, he knew better.

Aiden shook his head. "What in the world did he hit her with?"

Beau closed his eyes. "I don't know. Something weighty enough to do this. I don't even want to think about what would've happened if Level's friend hadn't heard her scream."

"Odd that he didn't mention the friend's name." Aiden sat in the chair the reverend had vacated.

"Maybe the friend asked that he not say who he was. We don't know. I trust the reverend. If he doesn't want to tell us, I'm all right with that."

Aiden nodded. "I think I'll run back to the house and let the girls know. Level's cart is pretty small for all of us and it's a short walk."

"Good idea. Have them get our bed ready for her." Beau continued tenderly combing Ruby's hair with his fingers. Aiden prayed they'd find Hattie, and his stomach met his boots when he thought about telling Jennie what had happened.

Chapter Thirteen

Jennie sat at the table with the rest of her sisters, drumming her fingers and waiting for any noise at all from outside. Eva laid her hand on Jennie's arm. "Do you think we should do anything while we wait? What if they don't come back tonight?"

"Please, don't say that. They have to come back and they have to find Ruby and Hattie." Jennie stood and collected two of the plates from the dinner that no one had touched.

Drawing hot water from the reservoir on the side of the cook stove, Jennie lathered some soap on a rag to wash the dishes. Eva brought in the rest of the plates and slipped them into the water. "I'll dry for you." She picked up a towel.

Eva hated change and had always been the sister who tried to keep the peace among all of them. She was generally so quiet, everyone would forget she was even there.

Jennie needed the quiet ritual of doing the dishes to let her mind settle, so having the quietest sister help her was the best option. She'd been too upset to eat. Why hadn't she tried harder to stop Ruby? While she'd sometimes thought about what things would've been like if Ruby hadn't brought them with her, she knew Ruby had sacrificed a lot to do it. She and Beau were newly married and both were filled with a wanderlust that normally might make having a family difficult, but they had agreed, even before they were married, that Ruby's sisters would be with them.

Jennie shook her head as she wrung out her washcloth. "Thank you, Eva. I'll dump this outside, then we should get ready for bed."

Eva nodded. A knock sounded on the front door and they both gasped and ran for it. Jennie lifted the wood slide of the peep hole. "It's Aiden!" she yelled, her spirit soaring with hope.

Jennie swung the door open and saw the weary smile on his face. She ran into his arms without thinking and he wrapped them around her, holding her tight. "Let's go inside and I'll tell you what I know." He whispered in her ear as he placed his hand on her back. Warmth spread over her, strengthening her. He indicated that Jennie and Eva should sit on the couch then knelt in front of Jennie.

"We found Ruby with Reverend Level. She was hit over the head and has a pretty bad bump. She won't be able to work for a few days once she wakes up."

He searched Jennie's eyes and she wanted desperately to know what he was trying to tell her.

"Hattie's gone. She wasn't with Ruby and we have no idea who took her, much less where. Level is going to ask around tomorrow and we hope to find out more. Beau is pretty shaken up about it."

Jennie shook her head, her thoughts spinning out of control. She reached out and clutched Aiden's hand. "No, she can't be gone." Jennie felt tears well up and made an effort to slow her breathing, but the more she tried, the worse it became, until her stays bit deeply into her and the tears fell anyway. "This is Beau's fault. He brought us all out here. He knew the danger and still brought us out here!"

Aiden stood and yanked her up off the couch and into his arms, tucking her head under his chin. "Don't say that. Beau couldn't have foreseen this. He told Ruby to stay in the house and for whatever reason, she decided not to.

But whatever your feelings, Ruby needs you to get her bed ready and manage the house. We'd planned to tell you all we're moving out to the ranch next week, but now everything's on hold."

Jennie pulled away from him. "We can't leave now! What if Hattie finds her way back and looks for us? She'll never find us out on some ranch. She'd look here first."

Aiden backed away. "It isn't for me to say, Jennie, or you. You'll need to do what Beau and Ruby decide."

"And what about you, where will you go?" Jennie crossed her arms, all the mixed feelings inside of her swirled and flashed, turning to an anger she couldn't manage.

"If Beau'll have me, I'd like to work out on the ranch for the next month until I can earn my money to go home. I can help Beau keep looking for Hattie if he wants, but we'll probably just take it to Seth Bullock. If anyone can find her, he can."

"What makes you think he's got time to look for one missing girl. He's got this whole mess of a town to look after." Fury knotted in her stomach at the injustice. They may never see Hattie again. Oh, how she hated Deadwood!

Aiden pulled her back into his arms and she clutched the fabric at his neck, letting her tears soak his shirt. The last

166

thing she'd said to Hattie hadn't been kind, they hadn't gotten along at all in the last few weeks. She should've listened to Hattie more, tried to understand more.

"It's going to be okay, Jennie-girl. We have to hope and pray that she's found and she's all right. That's all we can do."

She nodded and clung to his strong frame. His muscled arms held her close. They were a comfort she didn't expect.

"You two go on up and get Beau and Ruby's room ready. Send the other girls down so I can warn them. Level and Beau should be here soon."

As usual, Eva had been so quiet Jennie had forgotten she was even there and heat crawled up her cheeks at what Eva had witnessed. She didn't want to let go of Aiden. Resting in his arms was the safest she'd felt in weeks, but he was right. Her sisters needed her to be strong now, so she must. She pulled away and rushed up the stairs, sending the remaining four sisters down to talk to Aiden.

She'd never been in Beau and Ruby's room before. They hadn't had much in the way of privacy since their wedding night, so all the girls had a silent agreement that their room was off-limits. They needed someplace that was only for them. She pushed open the door and stood just outside. Even knowing she'd been told to enter, she didn't want to. Jennie stepped inside and cupped the side of the water pitcher. It was cool, but not cold. There was nothing in the bowl, so she didn't need to refresh anything.

She turned down the blankets and opened the armoire, pulling out a sleeping gown for Ruby. She heard the front door open and rushed back downstairs as Beau carried Ruby into the house, followed by the reverend. A white cloth wrap covered half of Ruby's face.

Beau carried her up the stairs and Jennie glanced around the living room, not sure what to do next. The reverend was on the couch and her younger sisters sat silently, their faces white and eyes wide. Aiden stepped in behind her and led her over to a chair. Her legs were stiff, as if they were frozen solid.

Level clasped his hands in front of him and bowed his head. "Lord, we seek your guidance today. We don't know why terrible things happen, but we know we are not promised an easy time, only peace. We need your peace now, Lord. The peace that will help us understand that you can reclaim all situations for good. We ask that my query tomorrow is fruitful and that if it be your will, young Hattie would come home quickly. Amen."

The group mumbled an 'amen' in response.

The reverend stood and pulled his vest down tight over his stomach. "Jennie, you'll have to take care of Ruby for a while. She won't be capable and, frankly, she might not be willing for a while. She might blame herself for Hattie's disappearance. Be gracious to her, help her." He turned to Aiden. "You said you were moving out to the Ferguson place next week?"

Aiden nodded, his steady hand remained on her shoulder. "Yes, that's right."

"I think you should go, do your work on the ranch, and let the sheriff and his men handle this, it's what the town pays them for. I had meant to be moving on here real soon, but if I find out anything tomorrow and it will help for me to stay, I will."

Aiden said, "Thank you, reverend. We'll take what help we can get. I didn't know Hattie all that well but I aim to help however I can before I leave."

The reverend cocked his head. "Where're you headed?"

"Kansas. That's where my family is, and I need to go back to settle a few things."

"It's good to keep with your family, except when you can't." He raised his eyebrows, smiled mysteriously at Aiden, and left.

169

Eva, Francis, Lula, Nora, and Daisy all moved to the couch next to Jennie or sat at her feet. They were silent, but each girl needed to be close to the others. Jennie touched each sister on the arm or head. "We'll get through this. We Arnsby's always do."

Eva gripped Jennie's hand. "What if Hattie never comes back? What if we never find her? She's my twin, like half of me." Eva's mouth quivered.

Aiden sat on the arm of the couch. "Please don't think that way, Eva. We're going to do our very best. It's only been a few hours. She couldn't have gone far. If we need to get the sheriff involved, like Reverend Level said, then we will. I'm sure they'll find her. We need to keep working. As much as we all want to, we can't just stop and spend every waking minute looking for her. Beau and I will go out and check a few of the... less savory establishments tonight. If she isn't there, we'll talk to the sheriff in the morning. If he directs us to the marshal, so be it. We'll do what we need to, to find her."

Eva shook her head. "They won't find her. Hattie was looking for a chance to get out. She wanted to see the world and meet all sorts of men. She wanted attention. Ma never knew it, but Hattie used to steal Pa's moonshine. When we first arrived in Cutter's Creek, Hattie had the sweats and the shakes. I didn't know she'd been nipping from Pa that much, but she was hooked. You'll find her where there are men and booze."

Jennie gasped. "Eva, don't say such things. From what Aiden was told, she was taken and that's what I'll believe until we learn otherwise. It isn't right to condemn our sister when she isn't here to defend her reputation."

Eva shook her head. "What reputation? She won't have one after tonight. You were there, you were next to her on the floor of the hotel the night of the fire when we lost Pa. I remember you asking Hattie if she had enough blankets because she was shaking like a leaf. Don't you remember how she avoided Ma for over a week? I don't think any of us knew the real Hattie until we got to Cutter's Creek and found out she *wasn't* very nice at all."

Jennie closed her eyes; Eva's words rang true. Hattie had been quite docile while they lived at home, and frequently liked to be alone in the small lean-to next to the house. She'd become angry as soon as they'd gotten to the hotel that first night, and from then on...

"While you may be right, Eva, let's wait to pass judgment. We all know living in that tiny house with Pa and his ways was hard. Hattie may not have found a good way to handle it, but it was a way."

Beau trudged down the stairs. "Jennie, Ruby is awake and she's asking for you."

Chapter Fourteen

Jennie raced up the stairs and into Beau and Ruby's room. She knelt next to the bed. Ruby's face was shocking and it took all Jennie's concentration not to flinch and gasp. "Ruby? It's Jennie, I'm here."

"Jennie?" Ruby reached out and groped for her hands as if she couldn't see. "I'm so sorry I didn't listen to you. It was a set up. Hattie had been talking to the man next door for a few days when she'd let Jack outside. She'd told him to watch for her if she ever got free of the house. I don't know what he offered her, but the plan never was to take me, only her. She wanted out. If I'd taken you instead, she would've left with him while I was gone and the girls

would've been alone. I wasn't bothered
at all until Hattie left me and climbed
into a wagon with the man who'd
knocked on our front door this morning,
and another man who looked a little familiar." She squinted. "But I don't know
why." She shook her head. "I screamed
for her to get down, I grabbed for her
and then he kicked me. I fell back and
would've been trampled by his horses,
but a man grabbed for me. When he did,
something else hit me above the eye and
I don't remember anything after that.
Maybe the horse kicked me." She gingerly rubbed the spot above where her
face turned a harsh purple.

Jennie combed the hair back out of
Ruby's face and tears welled up inside
her, pushing their way free. "A friend of
Reverend Level saw you and that's
where Beau and Aiden found you. I can't
believe Hattie would just run off..."

"I knew she was unhappy. She
wanted to get out, see the town, inves-
tigate. I could tell that something wasn't
right, but I didn't know what. I'd bet Ma
knew. I wish she would've warned me. I
could've kept a better eye on her."

"Oh, Ruby, what'll we do? She could
be anywhere. Do we go after someone
who doesn't want to be found? She's
only sixteen." Jennie's stomach turned
sour as terrible, worrying thoughts
flooded her.

"It won't be up to me. It'll be up to Beau, this's his household. Ma gave us complete control."

Jennie rested her chin on the bed to hide her face and calm herself. "We should've been able to choose between staying and going. I think most of us would've chosen to stay."

"That's exactly why we didn't. Ma couldn't provide for you and Mr. Williams certainly couldn't, either. He's not young and he can't work. Ma and I both agreed I would take you because Beau is capable of taking care of all of us. Even when we have a family of our own, you will still be just as loved and cared for."

"You don't think she'd try to go back to Cutter's Creek, do you?" Jennie knew the answer before she was even done asking the question. Hattie wanted freedom, and that meant from Ma, too.

"No. She didn't want to be with Ma any more than she wanted to be with me. She wants someone like Pa who'd provide her the hooch and leave her alone. Trouble is, I don't think she'll find anyone who'll leave her alone."

"You knew?" Jennie sat back away from the bed. How had Ruby known and no one else but Eva?

"Yes. Ma told me as soon as we got off the wagon when we arrived in Cutter's Creek. I'd seen how Hattie was shaking. I was worried she'd caught her death of cold.

Jennie let that idea roam in her head. "I'm worried about the men, too. Just how far will Hattie go to get what she wants?" A pain wedged itself deep in her heart; she knew what Hattie would do, she'd practically spelled it out with their last argument.

Ruby reached out and squeezed Jennie's hand. "I need to rest, but I wanted to tell you what happened before I forgot." She gently rubbed the angry bruise on her head. "Please, don't tell the other girls. I don't know how much they know and I don't want them to feel any less for Hattie. If she does come back, we need to love her, not condemn her."

"Eva already told everyone about Hattie's drinking. The others seemed quite ready to believe it. I think the only one in the dark was me."

Ruby laid her head back against the pillow. "I'm sorry to hear that. I wish Eva had confided her fears to me. Since they're twins, Eva was probably more observant of Hattie than any of us."

Jennie pulled the coverlet over Ruby and left the room.

Oh, Hattie. Why didn't you focus your attention on Aiden for a little longer? At least then you'd still be here. She knew Aiden had paid little attention to Hattie or any of her sisters. He knew their names, but the only one he ever spoke to was her.

Jennie wandered to the edge of the stairs and stopped, listening to Beau and Aiden as they spoke below her on the landing. She leaned over, grasping the wall for balance.

"Ruby told me Hattie wanted to go and that she left by wagon. She isn't around here. I'd rather not visit any of these places, especially if the only fruit that would come of it would be rotten," Beau remarked.

Aiden sighed. "I agree. If she wanted to go bad enough to take a wagon with some stranger, you aren't going to find her next door. I *do* think we should get the sheriff or the marshal involved."

"I agree, Aiden. I can't fathom what we did that would've made her run, but I pray the Lord's with her and we'll find her safe. I'm afraid Hattie has no idea how big and cold the world can be."

Jennie's feet thudded down the stairs as she struggled against the weight of moving at all. She'd misjudged Hattie completely. Beau and Aiden turned as she descended the last few steps.

"I'm sorry for listening." She searched their faces for any hint of anger, finding none, she went on. "I think you're right. I didn't want to believe it, but once Eva pointed out Hattie's changed behavior, I couldn't help but notice. I hope the sheriff finds her, but perhaps being on her own for a bit, of her own choice, will help her to see what a blessing family can be."

Aiden nodded and approached her. "Beau and I will be working tomorrow and Ruby is not to get out of that bed."

Jennie's hands felt clammy and she wiped them on her skirt. "I've never run the household. It's never been my place."

Aiden smiled at her and caressed her chin, lifting it slightly. "Now, that isn't the spitfire I met on the trail, who fell out of the wagon, 'cause she was so curious. That isn't the girl who gave as good as she got every time I teased her."

Jennie closed her eyes and stepped away from his gentle touch. She couldn't think straight, looking up into those penetrating eyes. "Life was easier, then."

"Jennie Arnsby, you are a strong and capable woman. I have no doubt you'll be just fine. You don't have to be perfect."

Beau stepped forward. "Thank you, Jennie. I know I can trust you to look after the place, and please keep the girls from bothering Ruby too much. I think she'll be back on her feet even before a doctor would want her to, but that's just her way."

Jennie turned from the men. "That it is. She's as stubborn as a goat. We all are, I'm afraid."

Aiden touched her shoulder and she turned to him. "We'll move out to the Ferguson place in three days. One way to keep the girls busy and not dwelling on Hattie is having them pack their things."

"There's so little to pack." Jennie shook her head. "I'll find something to do and we'll keep an eye out for Hattie. Maybe she'll change her mind and come home."

Aiden pulled her into an embrace and she held on to him tightly, accepting the strength and comfort he offered. "Don't let yourself dwell on it, I don't want your heart to break further." She felt his warm breath fan over her head and his lips pressed against her hair. Her heart tripped over itself but before she could even think to pull him back, he was gone.

Aiden turned and followed Beau out the door and the house went silent. She hurried to the back door and let Jack in before he could scratch a hole in the door. Holding it open, she searched the fence for any sign of the old man who'd spoken to her. The back door of the other house swung in the wind as if the house was abandoned. She wouldn't search the house for Hattie, but if anyone were there, surely, they would secure the door.

Jack nuzzled her hand and whined

for attention. She took Jack back inside and knelt next to him. "You'll help me tomorrow, won't you? I used to be strong, like Aiden said, but I've lost my way. I'm scared to make a wrong move or miss any sign my sisters are hurting."

Jack leaned in to her, enjoying the scratches behind his ears, and whining happily.

"Well, at least I know you'll help me watch the door."

Chapter Fifteen

Jennie helped her sisters into the two wagons as Beau and Aiden loaded their trunks. Ruby squinted into the sun and pulled on a hat, tying it off as she strode from the house to the lead wagon. Beau insisted she not drive the three miles to the Ferguson ranch, so she'd ride with him. That meant Aiden would be driving the other wagon, with her, Eva, and Lula.

Aiden rushed back into the house and returned to the wagon with a flour sack. He laid it under the seat and climbed up next to her.

"Are you ready for our next adventure?" His eyes twinkled. For a man who had no intention to stay, he sure enjoyed acting as part of the family.

"I don't know anything about ranching, but I'll be happy to go outside and enjoy a day again, and Jack will like being able to run free. I don't think he wanted to stay in the house that much." Jennie couldn't wait to have the room to stretch her legs when she wanted, and just get outside and breathe fresh air.

Aiden paused and his brow crinkled. "I'm sure you're right. I know we talked about it last week, but I don't think I can take him on the train to Kansas. If I were riding, it'd be different, he could just come with me. But I don't have a horse of my own, and I can't afford one."

Jennie nodded. "I wish I could keep him, Aiden, but it isn't my place. You'll have to talk to Beau. It'll be his house." She couldn't look at him, couldn't let him see the hope she had that he'd come back, even if it were just for the dog and not her.

Aiden nodded and his jaw hardened into a flat line. "We'll be living on a ranch with quite a few men... you won't go running off on me... will you?"

Jennie had to grip the side of the wagon seat or risk falling out in her shock. He'd never been quite so bold. "Aiden, I don't plan on running off with *anyone*. That just isn't the life for me."

"Good." He flashed a dazzling smile that left her belly fluttering. "Now that that's settled..." He flicked the lines to keep up with Beau's wagon. "Let's talk a bit. I've saved up enough working with Beau and doing extra work the last week, but I'm not quite ready to leave yet."

Jennie craned her neck to look him in the eye. "How did you manage to work enough to save a month's worth of wages in one week?"

"I talked to the boss. Whittling the blocks for the pictures was expensive work and takes a skilled hand. It paid more. I offered to do it." He shrugged a shoulder.

"I thought leaving was all you could think about. You said you weren't a man if you didn't make right whatever went wrong back home."

"That's true, but I'm worried my da won't take me back. I've failed, which is exactly what he predicted. I told him I'd be this great prospector and make all this money. He'd always been so proud of my brothers; I wanted him to be proud of me. I'd be more than happy to work for him to earn back his respect, but there won't be much to do until harvest. It would be best if I returned right when they need me. If I come before and there's no hard work to do, they may not welcome me back."

Jennie couldn't think of a single reason she wouldn't take back her own family, even her pa, who had been a reprobate, wasn't excluded. While she'd not want to live with him, she'd never wish him gone. "Do you really think they'd turn you out over a misunderstanding?"

Aiden frowned but didn't look at her. "I don't know. I can't say for sure. I just know I'd give about anything to take back the things I said before I left. I didn't even let my mam know I was leaving, I was in such an all-fired hurry." He shook his head. "I just hope they can forgive me, is all."

"I think you'll be surprised. Just like if Hattie would come home even now after only being gone a few days, we'd take her back immediately. She'd be forgiven for running off, for scaring us, and even for putting Ruby in danger."

"Not every family is as forgiving as yours, Jennie."

She sighed and allowed the rocking of the wagon to pull her from side to side. "I'll pray they forgive you and that you have a wonderful homecoming." *But I'll also pray that you want to return... someday.*

"I sure am going to miss you." He moved the lines to his left hand and touched her cheek gently with his right. His eyes were soft and tenderness welled within them.

She felt heat rise up her neck. "I'll miss you, too. How long do you think you'll be gone?"

He turned back to watching the

184

horses. "I don't know. Right after harvest comes the winter. It can be slow in coming in Kansas, or it can hit hard and early. It'll be colder here sooner than there."

"But if you're riding the rails, it shouldn't matter... right?" She needed to hear that he wouldn't be gone for too long. Somewhere between yanking on her braid and kissing her head... she'd fallen for him and, though he had to leave, it wouldn't be easy letting him go.

"If I aim to help Beau on the ranch, I really need to have my own horse. That means I'll be working for my da, if he'll have me, until I can earn one. It could take a while."

"But... what if the job with Ferguson isn't open when you come back? It isn't like you can expect him to hold it for you."

"I know. I guess I just hope Beau will want to hire me as soon as I'm able to return. I'll do my best. You know that, don't you?"

"I know you spend an awful lot of time looking at that Deadwood book and the rest of your time talking about returning to your folks. I don't fit in there anywhere. I don't love Deadwood. It took me away from a place I'd learned to think of as home, it took my freedom for a time, and it took my sister from me. I'm stuck in a place I detest because my sister's husband likes it."

Aiden shook his head. "None of those things have anything to do with Deadwood, they would've happened anywhere. If Beau had chosen anywhere else, you still would've had to stay inside until he learned that it was safe for his womenfolk to walk about. He was being a good protector and provider."

"That's easy for you, you're a man, you can walk about and do whatever you like."

"Not really. We have to work and bear the burden of making decisions. It isn't easy on us, either."

Jennie wanted to cross her arms, but she had to hold onto her seat on the bumpy trail.

"Why do you like to argue with me so much, Jennie-girl? I noticed you are sweet as apple pie to everyone else, but with me, you get sour as vinegar."

Jennie ducked her head to hide her embarrassment. It wasn't that she didn't like him, on the contrary, she liked him far too much. It was more that she felt secure with him, a freedom to be herself she didn't feel with anyone else. "I don't do any such thing."

"Whatever you say." He glanced over at her and gave her sly smile that said he could see right through her.

"You think you know me so well? You don't know one whit about me."

"Oh, really? I know you want to have

a say in everything. You always feel like because there are so many voices, yours isn't heard. I know that when you're nervous you tend to cut people off rather than face it. You don't like to confront people and you tend to put more weight on people's words than they mean." He narrowed his eyes and nodded. "Like when I said I couldn't find real riches here in Deadwood, that I'd have to go home to find them... you thought I was talking about you. I wasn't. As God as my witness, you're sitting next to me on this wagon which proves you are completely portable." He flashed her another glance then turned back toward the worn path.

"You're wrong, Aiden. I'm no treasure. If I'm gone, there are seven more just like me." She looked away from him, afraid he would see how much her own words hurt.

"That's not true one bit, either. Just like when you said Hattie had needs the rest of you didn't, so do you. I aim to find out what those are before I go."

"Why? You're leaving, Aiden. You may never come back. What if you're so happy with your family that you realize what you had here was fool's gold?" Her hands shook and she dug her fingers into the seat to keep them still.

Aiden pulled up on the lines and the horses came to a stop, pitching her forward until she locked her knees. Two heads popped up from the bed of the wagon behind them.

"You are not fool's gold, Jennie Arnsby, and if I knew for certain that you wanted to be with me, I'd ask Beau to court you proper before I go."

The two girls behind the seat erupted in gasps and giggles. They ducked back behind the seat in a fit of whispers.

Aiden sighed and reached out for Jennie's hand.

Jennie scooted back from him. "Well, I don't want you. I don't want a man who's going to leave and I won't split up my family any more than it already is!" She turned and climbed into the back of the wagon. Leaving her family after all they'd suffered wasn't possible. Losing Aiden would be horrible, but she couldn't lose her sisters. She glanced at Aiden's back. He slouched down in his seat and flicked the lines, nudging the horses faster to catch up to Beau and Ruby's wagon.

Aiden glanced behind him every few minutes, but Jennie wouldn't even gaze up at him... at least not when he was looking. He could feel her eyes boring a hole in his back. He scratched the back of his neck then stood up bracing his foot against the buckboard for balance. There were fences ahead, and fences meant people. They might have a mile or so to go, but they'd be there soon.

He flicked the lines and followed Beau diagonally up the side of a hill. His stomach flipped as visions of Jennie or one of her sisters falling out of the rig and tumbling down the hillside flashed through his mind. They called them the Black *Hills* but they were steep. The wagon slid on the loose rocks and the small granite chunks that marked the trail. Aiden pulled to the left and the horses veered off the trail to the right onto a level spot cut into the side of the hill, stopping the fall.

Aiden wiped his brow and let his breath catch up. There hadn't been any mangled wagons at the bottom and he didn't want to be the first. Beau had made it around the hill and was out of sight. Aiden flicked the lines and pulled right and the horses responded quickly, pulling them back onto the makeshift trail. The wagon lumbered around the bend. The closer they came to the top, the more the trail was made of little more than loose rocks.

As he turned the bend, a level area with a huge house and many outbuildings came into view. He followed Beau's wagon to the front of the house and stopped just behind it. He held the lines but turned in time to see Jennie helping the others out of the wagon. She didn't bother waiting for him.

He shook his head. That woman ran hot as fire and cold as ice and, somehow, she'd wheedled her way into his blood. Beau strode out of the house, followed by a man with salt and pepper hair and a thick mustache. Aiden met them as they stepped off the front porch.

The older man held out his hand. "You must be Aiden Bradly, I'm Brody Ferguson." He gave a firm shake then turned, spreading his arm out wide. "What's visible here on the ledge is about a tenth of the area I've got. You saw some of the fence coming in, but we've got enough land for pasturing. Beau, I see you traded your oxen for horses, that's good. You can't ride the range on no ox." He laughed. While Aiden couldn't tell which state he'd hailed from, his slight drawl pegged him as a former Southerner.

Beau chuckled. "That's the truth. Bradly, here, might only be staying for a few weeks. He's got business to tend to down in Kansas."

"Will you be returning after your business, or is the trip permanent?" Brody asked.

Aiden glanced at the women standing by the other wagon and crossed his arms over his chest. "I don't know for sure, sir. If I'm needed, I won't be able to return."

Brody nodded. "The job will always be here. I'll need men until this place folds, which I hope'll never happen. You get your business tended to, then send me a wire and tell me if you're coming back or staying there."

Aiden nodded. Leaving his new boss so shorthanded left a bad taste in his mouth, but without knowing if his da would welcome him back, he couldn't make any promises.

"You should get your horses put up for the night. I'm sure they're tired. I've got a few in the corral you can take. Saddle 'em up and I'll show you around the place. We won't be back until supper. You'll all be eating with us tonight. Lefty had to go buy some provisions in Lead, it's a little closer to us than Deadwood, but we're considered part of Deadwood."

He pointed to a spot behind the house. "That log house yonder, with the red door, that's your place, Beau. Aiden. I don't have a bunkhouse built yet, but I do have a small cabin my ma used to live in about twenty yards behind the log house. That one's yours."

"Thank you, sir." Aiden tipped his hat and he and Beau led the teams to the large stable.

"Beau, tell me something... are *all* the Arnsby girls stubborn?" Aiden brushed the dust from the horse's mane.

Beau shook his head. "Aiden, you don't know the half of it. Have you finally got up the gumption to ask me to court Jennie?"

"I'd like to, but she said no. Said she doesn't want to if I'm going to leave. I want to come back. I like it here. Jennie's a formidable woman, but if I can't break through that layer of anger... If she don't want me here, I don't see any reason to leave my da if he needs me."

"Let me tell you a little something about those sisters. Their pa threatened them with sorry marriages from the time they were very young. He wanted them all gone, would've traded every last one of them for one boy. With the exception of Hattie, not a one of them is interested in getting married."

Aiden frowned. "Beau, you're married to one. Obviously, they aren't *that* opposed to it."

"For Ruby, I had to prove I wanted her heart and that I'd do anything, including let her go, to show her how much she meant to me."

Aiden led his horse to the stall and poured some oats in a trough. "I'm not following you, Beau. You let her go?

What does that mean?"

"Ruby was as timid as a rabbit any time she was near me, ran away from me at every turn. I finally had to prove to her I wasn't hunting her down, but I'd do anything for her, including saving her sisters from their father, which we did."

"Well, I can't rescue everyone and I know bringing Hattie back would help, but I wouldn't even know where to begin."

"It isn't that easy, Aiden. You need to talk to her, find out what it is that's the most important thing, then help her get it."

"That ain't going to be easy."

Beau laughed as he closed the gate for the last horse. "If it was easy, every man would be married. Let's go pick out a horse. Don't want to keep the new boss waiting."

"You really think I can get her to stop running?"

"If you're intentions are honorable and you keep trying... yes. And Aiden, don't you go laying your lips on my Jennie again until you get permission to court her."

He smiled as the approached the corral. "Can I have permission just in case?"

Beau raised a warning eyebrow. "Just in case, what?"

"Just in case she changes her mind."

Beau's let his eyebrow fall. "I'll give you permission to court, but that's as far as it goes for now."

Aiden smiled as the afternoon sun lit golden pockets through the trees. "Yes, sir." The day was looking better by the minute.

Chapter Sixteen

Jennie paced back and forth in front of the empty stove. This house was smaller than the last two, but would fit them just fine as long as she didn't need room to breathe or think. But there was the problem, she needed to do both and there just wasn't enough space. There was one large open room for a parlor, dining area and kitchen, a door separated the one bedroom on the main floor which would be for Beau and Ruby, and a large one room loft for all the girls. They even had a dresser, which they'd never had before, but that was the extent of the house.

Ruby rested in her room after the trip and the younger girls had put away their clothes. Jennie was restless with nothing further to do. She'd seen the whole cabin and wanted to explore, but none of the men had bothered to tell the women if they could. They'd arrived hours ago and the soft light of evening poured through the windows. She needed air or she'd suffocate on the spot.

Aiden's cabin was empty and he hadn't had a chance to unpack since he'd had to work right away. She could go and spruce it up for him. He'd gotten used to her fussing over him back in Deadwood so it would be no bother to make sure his tick was ready and that he had water to wash up with when he returned. It would give her something to do and get her away from the walls that were moving in on her with every breath.

She slipped out the back door so she wouldn't disturb Ruby, and Jack followed her. When the door was shut and she began her walk, he jumped and barked, chasing every scent and enjoying his new freedom.

"You'll have to stay over at Aiden's now. You're not my dog, Jack."

His large fuzzy head tilted at an odd angle then he scampered away.

Jennie came to the small cabin in short order and pushed the door open. Inside, every bit of space was used, a corner for the bed, the cook stove sat along one wall, with one small cupboard for eating and cooking utensils. She closed the door behind her and smiled at the sweet space, taking in the tiny kitchen area. *It isn't like he'll use that, I'm sure he'll eat with us ... until he leaves.*

The coverlet on the bed was dusty so she took it outside to the clothesline and hung it over, beating the dust out with a long stick. When she'd freshened it up a bit, she took it back inside and made the bed. The wash bowl next to the bed was dry so she pumped some water for him, careful not to spill anything on the floor or it would be difficult to sweep.

She heard a squeak and turned as a large man filled the doorway. His long coat billowed out around him and his hat shaded his face. With the sun behind him, she couldn't see who it was and she gasped. Trapped inside Aiden's cabin.

"Jennie-girl? What're you doing in my house?" He swung his hat from his head and tossed it on the table. As he stepped inside, she could see heat and confusion warring in his eyes.

Jennie breathed deeply and licked her suddenly dry lips. "I thought ... you might like it if I freshened the place up a bit. I'm sorry if I was intruding." She stepped to the side and dashed for the door. His lean arm snaked out and caught her around the waist, tugging her close to him.

"Jennie-girl, promise me you won't ever go into a man's house alone again unless you're married to him. I don't want to see you hurt and other men might not be thankful as I am."

"Well, of course I won't just go into a man's home. You must not think very much of me if you do." Strange that she had no desire to fight against his hold, even though what he'd said made anger bubble like acid in the back of her throat.

His voice dropped to a whisper next to her ear and she shivered. "Oh, I think far too highly of you. But right now, I need you to scoot out of here before anyone sees you or we'll both be in trouble." He swatted her on the behind with his free hand to get her going.

Of all the insufferable things a man could do, she blustered and fussed, making him laugh. He turned around so she couldn't see his face.

"Aren't you gone yet?"

"Mr. Bradly. I'll thank you to keep your hands off me." Her heart raced as he slowly turned and strode up to her each step painfully intent. He put his hands behind his back and leaned down. His breath fanned her cheek and she closed her eyes. Her skin tingled and she gripped her own hands behind her back to keep from grabbing the front of his shirt and dragging him in closer. His scent was straw, leather, and work and it had never thrilled her more. He pressed his lips against hers and her breath caught in her throat, pulling back as the pleasant feeling of anticipation burst through her. She flung her eyes open.

"You didn't say anything about my lips." He laughed.

She gathered her skirts and rushed out the door, his laugh chasing her down the trail.

Jennie rushed through the log cabin's back door and washed her hands, splashing cool water on her face.

Ruby laughed and all her embarrassment came back. Had Ruby seen where she'd come from? "Jennie! Where have you been? I looked around for you, but didn't see you anywhere."

Jennie turned and dried her face with the towel. "I was..." Aiden's words of warning rang in her ears. "I was just looking around outside."

"Well, you weren't here to hear Beau's warning. They spotted some strange hoof prints up on the north hill pasture. He asked that we stay close to the houses. We're free to roam about here, but not to wander too far."

"I won't wander. It is beautiful out here ... reminds me a little of Cutter's Creek." Anything to keep Ruby from asking about the heat that wouldn't leave her face.

Ruby glanced out the window and her face softened. "It does. I love the green of the trees, and from the top of this hill, it's like you can see for miles."

"That's true. Cutter's Creek was at the base of the mountains, but we're higher here, like you're a little closer to God."

Ruby turned back to her. "Jennie, I had a lot of time to think while I was resting and I'd be lying if I didn't tell you that Eva told me about your argument with Aiden on the way here... and what he offered. I'm worried you'll pass up the opportunity to be with him because of Hattie. Please don't let her choices ruin yours. If I could go back and change anything, I would've insisted Ma come with us. Hattie may not have run away from her, but we'll never know for sure."

"Ruby, this wasn't your fault and you can't go back so it doesn't do anyone any good to think on it." Jennie turned and splashed her face, one last time, to make sure any visible sign of Aiden's kiss was gone.

Ruby stepped toward her and rested her hand on Jennie's shoulder. "Jennie, I want you to think about something, deeply. You've based all your ideas on marriage on Ma and Pa, but they aren't your only guide. Think of Beau and I. Marriage can be a beautiful thing."

"I'm sure it can be... when you want it. I've been afraid of it for so long, how do I just change how I feel?" The thought of Aiden's lips on hers, just a few minutes before, sent heat crawling back up her cheeks. What would that kiss have become if she hadn't jumped back? They had been alone in his home...

"You first have to *want* to change, then you make decisions that slowly take you out of where you're comfortable. Love, in the beginning, isn't comfortable. It can be exciting and a little scary."

"I've spent the last year changing. I just want to find somewhere I can do my work and be left alone." Jennie had to get away from Ruby. Ruby would never understand that she *did* love Aiden, but she couldn't let herself hope until he returned. She rushed up the ladder, in the loft to change for supper. The longer Aiden was here, the more everyone would try to push them together. He certainly made her pulse race when he got close, or when he teased her, but feelings just weren't enough. Ma had talked about the feelings she'd had when she first met Pa, and *she'd* ended up living in a tiny house with eight girls and a husband who brewed moonshine. Feelings couldn't assure her Aiden would return. Until then, his parents came first.

She pulled her work dress over her head and changed into her one nice ecru lace dress. She buttoned the front up the high neck and looked down at it. While it wasn't elegant, it fit her well after her alterations. She helped Lula with her braids and gathered the girls to come down. They would go over to the main house for supper as a family.

Jennie held her skirts close to her and climbed down the ladder from the loft. When she reached the third rung from the bottom, someone grasped her waist and swung her down. She turned and Aiden's hands squeezed her waist gently, fitting comfortably and almost encircling her back and belly.

"You look beautiful, Jennie-girl." He beamed down at her and she froze, not sure what to say or do. He'd shaved and put on a shirt she didn't recognize. It was clean and white and looked so nice with his brown leather vest. His sandy red hair was just a bit too long and she wanted to push it behind his ears.

Beau cleared his throat and Jennie jumped away from Aiden for the second time that day. Aiden chuckled and offered her his arm.

"Care to walk with me?"

If she refused, she'd look rude in front of everyone... if she accepted, it

202

was almost an acceptance of his pursuit. She hesitated, then reached out and touched his arm. For now, she would avoid *saying* she accepted him.

He grinned at her and swept her from the cabin. When they were outside and a few steps ahead of everyone else, he laid his hand on hers.

"Thank you for freshening up my cabin. I should've said so when I got there."

Jennie tried to pull her hand back, but his held hers firm. "As I recall, your lips were too busy with other things for the task."

His hazel eyes darkened to the color of a beautiful glade. "Aye, and don't tell me you wouldn't rather have that than a thank you." His voice was thick, intimate. She shivered.

"That's what I thought. It was just such a pleasant shock to find you there. A man doesn't expect to find a beautiful woman waiting for him unless he's married to her."

Jennie watched her feet as she walked across the sparse grass. "I was only trying to be kind. I didn't even mean to be there when you returned."

"I'm not complaining. In fact, I'm hopeful someday I can come home to you every day."

Jennie shook her head. "Aiden, stop. I enjoy your company, more now than I did at first, for sure, but I'm not interested in marriage. Not now... or ever. I've always seen marriage as a threat, something held over my head. I'm not going to choose it, ever." That's what she'd keep telling him so it didn't hurt so terribly when he left. Maybe if he believed it, so would she, but it didn't stop the words from tearing something within her.

Aiden held her hand on his arm as they stepped onto the porch and waited for Beau. She saw the confusion in his eyes and he stepped away from her, and a coldness filled the space like a wall. She swallowed back the words to bring him back to her. The sooner she got her heart to forget him, the better off they would both be. *He was leaving.*

Beau led Ruby and the five other sisters onto the porch, Eva trailing silently at the rear. Beau knocked and a Chinese woman opened the door.

She spoke with clipped words. "Mr. Ferguson is waiting. This way." She closed her eyes and bowed her head slightly. A few silver strands ran through her thick black hair tied back in a large bun. Her tiny feet made soft swishing noises under the strange robe she wore, like a long coat, as she led them in short steps to the sitting room. Jennie knew the woman was Chinese because there was a group of Celestial's settled in Deadwood, but she'd never actually seen one.

The woman stopped in front of a set of large double pocket doors and gestured inside. Jennie hesitated for a moment, wanting to know more about the woman but would her host think her rude for her curiosity? Jennie tilted her head to the side and waited as the others entered the room.

"Something wrong, young one?" the woman asked.

Mr. Ferguson approached them, smiling. "This is my housekeeper, Mrs. Chen. She lost her husband a few years ago and has been with me for some time. She used to work in the laundry seven days a week, twelve hours a day. It wasn't right, so now she's here."

Jennie held out her hand. "It's nice to meet you, Mrs. Chen."

She looked at Jennie's hand and nodded, then turned to the back of the house leaving them.

Mr. Ferguson put his hand at Jennie's waist and directed her in the room. "Don't take her lack of reaching out as a refusal to get to know you. Lei was treated very poorly in Deadwood and is still suspicious of people. Her people work hard in the laundries and mines, but folks are scared of what's different.

Jennie whispered, "What happened to her feet?"

"That's their custom. I don't know

205

the whole story, just that many of the women there have those tiny feet. In fact, those that don't are often unmarried and ridiculed."

"Strange." Lei came from a life completely foreign from her, one not embraced by others in the community. Hadn't Beau said Chinatown was dangerous? Lei certainly didn't seem so. She wanted to follow Lei instead of sitting in a boring dinner, talking about cattle.

"It is, but strange isn't always bad. And, while I don't share the fears of some of the people in Deadwood, I do understand. Before they moved west, many of them heard of the dangers of *different* people. They've been taught to fear those who believe differently, have different rituals and ways. Without more people willing to cross the lines we create, our worlds will remain shared, but separate."

Lei appeared at the end of the hall and slowly made her way toward them, stopping just a few feet away. She bowed her head and waved down the hall as a short man pushed a cart laden with plates.

"Thank you, Mrs. Chen. You need not serve us. You may have the rest of the evening off. Thank you for staying."

Lei nodded and folded her hands in front of her as she made her way past them and back to the front of the house.

"Isn't it difficult for her to move around?" Jennie wanted to know more.

"While she does have some difficulty, especially by the end of a day, she likes to remain helpful. I've offered her other jobs that would keep her off her feet. This is the one she wants to do the most. Now, let's turn our thoughts to something else, like the ranch. The Bar F was one of the first ranches near Deadwood. The railroad just started moving cattle this far northwest and I was glad to finally be doing what I wanted to. I'd heard all the stories about Deadwood and was fascinated. I came up here thinking I would stake a claim, strike it rich, and live out my days in luxury." He laughed.

Jennie shifted her gaze to Aiden, who was, for once, ignoring her and paying attention to Mr. Ferguson. Kindred spirits looking for wealth from the earth. She mentally shook off her pique that he could be so easily turned.

Mr. Ferguson's glance landed briefly on each guest. "The good Lord had other plans for me. I had the money to buy up four claims, all connected, not a single one of them had any dust that I could find, but it was prime land for cattle. I helped out a friend who had a reasonably good find of copper and he shared some of his earnings from selling his claim with me, which is how I was able to buy my cattle. I paid him back after the first year. Now, I don't need gold. I have a commodity that's even more rare than gold up here. Beef."

Aiden smiled. "So, you've been here a few years. Is the weather good for ranching?"

"Well, that remains to be seen. I've seen some wicked storms up here, but they don't come around every year. Everywhere you go, there're dangers to ranching, but cattle aren't much different than bison. They do have less hide, though, so you've got to move them into more protected areas when the weather starts to turn."

Aiden glanced at Jennie and caught her watching him. She dropped her gaze to her lap, her stomach tightening like a child's windup toy.

"Mr. Ferguson, it sounds and looks like you have a great spread here, with a lot of potential. I wish I could promise you that I'd be able to come right back from my travels. I wish I didn't have to leave at all."

His words slammed into her ears and she snuck a glance at him to see a mischievous smile directed at her. The room was suddenly stifling in her high-necked gown.

"Now, Aiden," Brody leaned on the table over his crossed arms. "I understand why you want to go, and why you might not come back. Don't concern yourself with it. I'll be showing Beau around for the next few days and after that, he'll be in charge of the hiring here. He's the one you'll need to prove yourself to if you return."

Beau sat up as the man from outside the door pushed a cart into the room and set heavily laden plates in front of each of them. Jennie eyed foods in front of her and didn't recognize most of it. She'd never seen so much food on one plate before, it overwhelmed her senses. Was she truly supposed to eat it all? She glanced around the table and her sisters were doing much as she was, unsure of what to do next. Brody folded his hands and bowed his head and they all followed. He said a short prayer over the food and then lifted his fork.

Ruby leaned over to Jennie and whispered in her ear. "It's beef. Beau bought it for me once. It's good, try it. You may not get a chance again for a long time." She straightened and started on her own meal.

Jennie reached for her knife and cut off a small bite. While the taste was similar to the venison she'd had growing up, it wasn't quite the same. She took a few more bites and knew she'd love to eat it again, given the chance.

The meal ended and she and her sisters were excused to leave. Ruby stayed with Beau so Jennie and Aiden led the girls back to the cabin. There wasn't much to say during their walk, their argument from earlier hung in the air like a wet sheet dividing them. Jack met them halfway and circled them, barking, then he ran off returning quickly, enjoying his freedom from four walls. Jennie turned and Aiden leaned over, patting Jack on the head.

The girls giggled as they ran into the house and watched from the front window. Jennie remained outside, waiting to see what Aiden would say or do. His revelation at dinner had been shocking, but perhaps no more than hers before. He smiled as he walked alongside her, past her house and under a tall spruce tree. He turned her to face back toward her house and looked up at the sky. The stars overhead were bright and the air was cool and calm, so fresh and clean after life in the city.

"So, what did you think of dinner?" He tucked her hand under his arm and held it there with light pressure as he gazed up at the stars. As she turned to see what fascinated him so in the sky her neck tingled with his warm breath. His gaze had drifted much further south than the heavens.

"It was pleasant. I learned a lot about the Chinese people of Deadwood."

"There's always more to learn. I know, if you get curious, you'll find a way to learn more. I'm happy to see you take some interest in Deadwood, even if it isn't a typical one."

She didn't want to argue with him; arguing over something so unimportant seemed silly and they'd already wasted enough of that day fighting. He'd only be with her another few weeks.

She shivered and stepped away from his arm. "Take me for a walk? I'm not supposed to go past the buildings alone." It seemed the perfect excuse to stretch the evening for a few extra minutes.

He gazed down at her, the darkness shadowing his face. She stopped, holding her breath. Perhaps she shouldn't have asked.

"I don't think it's a good idea to take you beyond the buildings or anywhere into the dark. A man has to know his limits, Jennie. If you want to see the stable and the buildings, I'll show them to you, in the morning."

She hadn't even considered what people might think of them wandering in the dark alone, but the sky was so perfect, the air so crisp. She'd been inside a house for too long. A short walk couldn't hurt.

"Are you always so concerned with what other people think?" She continued along the worn path ignoring his warning, toward the stables.

He sighed and turned to follow her.

211

Exasperation thickening his voice. "There isn't anyone out here to see us, which is part of the problem. I was thinking more of my *own* temptations."

She slowed her pace. "Well, maybe it would be best if I didn't go with you, then." If she let herself be alone with him in the barn would he take liberties and kiss her again? Would she mind if he did?

He laughed as he came alongside her. "I can probably keep myself in check for a few minutes, can you?" He tugged gently on her ear lobe and ran off into the stable.

Jennie clutched her skirts in hand and ran after him, laughing as she skidded to a stop just inside the door of the lighted barn. There was nothing to the left or right, it was as if he'd just disappeared. There was a row of horse stalls just to her right, most of them full. She leaned over and glanced down the row, then crept to the next. This row had empty stalls, the perfect place for him to hide.

She gingerly tip-toed over the rough concrete block floor, careful to check each stall. Her heart pumped in her ears as she waited for him to jump out and scare her, that would be just his way. She'd almost reached the end when a few blades of straw rained softly down on her head. She peered up as Aiden sat on a beam above her. His thickly muscled arms held him for a moment as he swung down then he extended them, releasing his body from the rafters above. He landed right in front of her and she gasped, nose to nose with him. His hazel eyes swept over her face, stalling on her lips, then he turned from her and scraped his hand over the back of his neck expelling a huge breath. She wanted to stalk over there and yank him back, she wasn't done with him yet.

"We shouldn't be out here. Brody showed us the tracks of unshod horses out in one of his pastures. Could be Indians or someone trying to look like Indians to stir up trouble. I should get you back home. It was foolish of me to bring you out here."

He grasped her arm and tugged her along with him. She lost her footing and slid along for a moment until she gained her feet and yanked herself free.

"Just wait one minute! You haven't shown me anything except that you know how to hide." Her breath ached to be free of her stays, she was breathing too hard to calm herself.

He returned to her, just a bare few inches away. "You don't understand, *M'fhíorghrá*. I can hardly stand to breathe if I'm not with you, but I know you'll never want to be with me, so I have to stay away. You're tearing me apart."

He closed the distance between them and nuzzled her ear. She leaned in closer, a sigh escaping her before she could pull it back. She let his breath fan her neck and the tension in her own belly tightened.

"What does that mean, what you called me?" Her voice was barely a whisper as she tilted her head to let him explore her neck further.

He nibbled below her ear, leaving a trail of heat. She'd never experienced anything so delicious.

"It's what my da always calls my mam." He took a step closer and his voice caressed her as sure as his hands on her shoulders and his mouth on her neck. "My da and mam's parents came to America to escape the Great Famine in Ireland. They found jobs in New York and raised their children together." He stopped and stepped back from her. His eyes hotter than his touch. "No one was surprised when my parents married. They'd been together their whole lives. What my grandparents *didn't* expect was that they would pull together the few dollars they could and move to Kansas." He shifted his body and laid his forehead against hers, breathing deeply. Her body pulsed, fanning a flame deep inside her. He was far too close and yet not close enough. She told her fingers to keep still but they wound their way around his waist against her will.

"My parents told us that leaving New York hurt our grandparents greatly, but there was nothing for them there but poverty. They weren't expecting their son to do as they did... leave without warning."

His words were full of so much pain and torment. She was tormenting him, keeping him from his purpose. "And that's why you have to go back." She breathed in the clean scent of the soap he'd used, the hay all around them, the oil he'd used on his leather vest. All the scents swirled about her, pressing themselves into her memory because, though he wanted to come back, it was never a guarantee and he *needed* to go home to be the man he wanted to be.

"Yes. I was young and foolish. I truly thought I could find better than what they gave me. If I didn't feel like I had to do this, I'd stay here. I would've not only asked Beau to court you, but I'd ask him for your hand just so I could be sure no other man could *ever* take you from me. Please understand, Jennie. This is something I feel like I have to do, like my soul is calling me home."

She stepped out of his arms and took his hands in hers. "If you're being called home, then you should go. Perhaps you'll feel tugged back here, but if you don't..." She couldn't finish. Her words choked her and she rushed past him out

of the stable and into the night. Her
tears ran down her cheek, blurring her
vision. She didn't know the lay of the
land well enough to run home from the
wrong end of the barn and Aiden soon
caught up to her.

He took her arm and turned her
around, holding her close. "It will be all
right. I'll be here for the next week to
show Beau I can learn quickly. That
way, if I return, I can just jump right
back into work."

He threaded his hand behind her
neck and held her close. She clutched
his vest in one hand and wove her other
in the hair at the nape of his neck but
it couldn't dispel what that one word did
to her heart... *if*. He held her close, her
forehead to his lips, until her tears ran
dry. He kissed the tears from her eye-
lashes then let her go.

"It's late. I'm sure Beau and Ruby
are back by now. I need to get you
home."

She nodded, unable to speak.

He led her to her door and opened it
for her. She stopped in the doorway.

"Good night, Aiden."

"Good night, M'fhíorghrá. "

Chapter Seventeen

Aiden strode into the barn just as the morning rays peered through the windows. The sunlight held bits of dust and warmed the stable floor as the horses stomped, wanting their freedom out in the pasture. He could understand their plight. He felt tied to returning to his parents, but like them, he didn't have a choice. He could only pray his da would let him free after, even if it meant working to return every cent he'd promised before he left.

Beau glanced up from the saddle he was fixing. "Morning. You're on time. That's a good start. It'll be easier in the future if you don't keep Jennie out so late."

Aiden heard Beau's meaning loud

and clear. "Yes, sir. What are we aiming for today?"

"Brody asked us to head out to those prints we saw yesterday, see where they lead. You up for a day in the saddle?"

Aiden nodded. "I better be if this's what I aim to do."

"Yup, you'll find yourself in the saddle more often than not. Brody said you should take Blaze, that roan down the second row. After the trip out yesterday with the heavy wagons, he didn't think any of the horses we brought were up to the task of riding all day."

Aiden nodded and went to the tack room. An old man sat on a bench oiling a saddle.

"What can a get for ya?" He looked up, his pipe hanging loosely from a jaw without enough teeth.

"I'm looking for a saddle for Blaze."

The old man laughed dryly and he caught his pipe as it fell from his mouth. "That one, right in front of you is the only one that'll work. He likes to flip ya, so be sure you're cinched good before ya' mount."

Aiden nodded. Testing the greenhorn was the way of things. He'd been tested when he started prospecting and he'd expected it here, too. Give the new guy the toughest horse, or the ugliest job, and see how well he could do it. Even if he's horrible, if he didn't give up, he'll eventually be good. That was just the way of it.

He cinched the saddle, then waited to the count of twenty-five, then pulled it tighter. He tested the stirrup and it didn't slide. Blaze turned out to be a good mount, easy to read. He took his cues well as Aiden took him for a trot around the corral. He patted Blaze on the neck and waited for Beau to mount and ride out.

They rode along the ridgeline for a while then cut north down into a valley. In the mud, along what had been a shallow creek during the snow melt, they found the tracks from the day before.

"This can't be Indians, it'd be too easy to find them," Beau said, dismounting and bending to take a closer look at the tracks. "They're excellent trackers and they wouldn't ride their horses down the one spot that would leave a trail. And if there had been water then, from the melt, it would've washed them away."

Aiden joined him next to the creek bed and squatted for a closer look. The middles of the tracks were damp, but the edges were dry and they were deep, too deep for a horse without a rider. It had been wet when the horses went through. "I agree with you, but why would people go to the trouble of finding unshod horses, to walk up this muddy spot just to stir trouble?"

"My guess is, they're planning to rustle a few cattle and hope Brody blames the Indians. If he does, he won't go looking to get them back." Beau shaded his eyes and gazed farther up the creek bed. "They were headed this way. Let's follow carefully and see if we can tell where it leads. My guess is, once this line of mud meets a lake or another river, we'll have lost them."

Aiden wiped his brow with his bandana. "I'm sure you're right, but if Brody wants us to check it out, then we'd best do it."

They mounted and followed the prints to a wash where the creek had become deeper. It carved a deep muddy groove between two hills. The hoof prints ended there.

"They came up on the grass right here. We'll ask Brody who owns the claim next to his. He can check with them and see if they've spotted the same signs."

"Or if they have an abundance of unshod horses." Aiden smirked, turning his horse back toward the ranch.

"There's always that chance, but let's hope we have better neighbors than that." Beau turned his horse as well. Blaze followed with little direction and Aiden used the chance to keep an eye out on the ridge for anyone watching them. They'd made it back to the area

220

where they'd first spotted tracks when Aiden heard a crack. Pain exploded in his shoulder, spreading flame through his arm and chest.

"Get down!" Beau yelled.

Aiden tried to reach for the reins but a black ring formed all around him, closing in on him. He felt his head meet the ground as he tumbled off his horse.

Jennie heard a shot—it was faint, but it made her jump. She'd expected to leave the shooting behind when they'd left Deadwood. Someone pounded on their door and Ruby rushed to answer it. She pulled the door wide and Brody stood outside panting and bent at the waist from his run.

Brody clutched the door jamb with one hand and his gut with the other. "Has Beau come back yet?"

"No, sir. They left early this morning and didn't come home for the noon meal."

Brody shook his head. "I'll have to take Lefty with me and see if we can find them. I heard a shot coming from the ridge where I sent them, and I don't think Aiden was armed, only Beau."

Jennie's heart sank into her feet. *No!*

"Ruby, what should we do? What if one of them is hurt? How should we get ready?"

Jennie turned in a circle, thinking of all the things they might need but unable to move from her spot to go get them.

Ruby touched her shoulder. "First, you're going to take a deep breath. Then you're going to go put clean sheets on my bed. No matter if one, both, or neither of them were hurt, we want to be ready and the only bed available is ours."

Jennie nodded, took a deep breath, letting it clear her mind, then dashed for the linen cupboard. Lei had made sure everything in their cabin was ready for them. Jennie grabbed what she needed and stripped Ruby's bed, remaking it with the clean bedding. She leaned out the door. "Do you think one of us should ride to Deadwood for a doctor?"

Ruby had begun heating water and she called from the stove, "No, not until we're told to. I don't know what Brody does out here for medicine, but it'd be a long ride all the way back to town. If it were a bad shot, they wouldn't live long enough for us to get there and back again."

Jennie felt sick and waiting made it worse. She paced in the living room until Ruby sent her outside. She walked to the stable. If she knew how to ride, she could go out herself and find out what was going on. She heard three more shots, all close together, and ran to the back of the house, watching the ridge behind the corner of Aiden's house.

Within a few minutes, she saw three riders and a horse clear the ridge and race toward her. One of the riders had another draped in front of him. He looked dead. Jennie sank to her knees. *No, Lord. No. Please don't take either Beau or Aiden... I'm begging you.*

The horses bore down on her, racing toward the safety of the ranch house and buildings. She ran back to the house and through it, avoiding Ruby as she dashed through the front door. Brody slid to a stop near her, tossing gravel and dust in her face, then dismounted. She couldn't take her eyes off the man draped over the front of his saddle. She knew the brown oil coat and saw the growing red spot down the sleeve. Tears erupted behind her eyes and her hands shook.

Brody broke through her frozen thoughts. "He's alive. Open that door, girl, so I can get him in and patched up before he bleeds out."

Jennie shook herself and ran for the door as Brody heaved Aiden over his shoulder and carried him into the house. Ruby rushed into the bedroom

223

and Brody laid Aiden on the bed as gently as possible. Aiden sucked in his breath and flailed as he hit the mattress. Jennie came close and brushed the sweaty hair from his head. He was shivering even with the heat of midsummer and her heart ached to take away his pain.

"How do we get his coat off without moving his arm?" She looked to Ruby, but Brody answered. "Go to the main house and ask Lei for the medical bag. I have a scissors inside that'll cut it. I had to move him more than I'd like just to get him here without any extra holes. I don't want to risk that ball causing any more damage."

Ruby dug through her bag and came up with the same scissors she'd used to cut Aiden's boots. She handed them to Brody as Jennie turned and ran from the house. The longer she stayed in Deadwood, the more she hated it. It took Hattie and now it could take Aiden, too. She pounded on the door to the house and it seemed to take a full minute for Lei to get to the door. She opened it slowly and gave Jennie a strange look.

"Mr. Ferguson not here. You go find him." She pushed the door against Jennie.

"No, wait, Mrs. Chen! Mr. Ferguson asked for his medical bag. Aiden's been shot!"

The woman hesitated then nodded. "You go."

Jennie glanced back at the cabin and then at Lei as she padded softly across the floor and out of sight. Jennie dashed back to the cabin, her lungs on fire, praying that Lei understood and would bring it.

"Lei is on her way with the bag, I think." Jennie gasped and bit her lip. She wished she'd been able to get better confirmation out of the woman.

"Good. She's as good as any assistant I've had. Now, as soon as she gets here, I want you two out. Nothing you say will make me change my mind on that. I'll have all the help I need with Beau and Mrs. Chen. Understand?"

Jennie touched Aiden's cheek. "But..."

"No."

Jennie closed her eyes against the fear of losing him, not to Kansas or his parents where he might return to her, but something much more permanent. She leaned over and kissed Aiden's forehead, her heart beating a terrible rhythm.

She whispered for his ears only. "You better not leave me, Aiden Bradly."

Mrs. Chen entered the log cabin without knocking and appeared at Brody's side.

Brody nodded to Ruby and Jennie. "Now, go."

Beau had been standing in the corner. He came forward and kissed Ruby on the head then gave her a squeeze. He whispered. "I'll tell you what happened later."

She kissed him on the cheek then ushered Jennie from the room. They sat on the couch in front of the empty fireplace.

"What if he doesn't make it, Ruby?" Her feet wanted to get up and pace but Ruby held her fast to the seat.

"That's a good question, Jennie. What *if* he doesn't make it? What would you do?"

Her throat clogged at the thought. "I know it doesn't do any good, but I keep praying God would take me instead."

Ruby draped her arm over Jennie's shoulder and pulled her close. "A wise friend once told me love had nothing to do with all those wonderful feelings you get when you're near one another. It has everything to do with wanting the very best for that person, even risking your own life to save them..."

"Are you saying I love him?" Jennie tucked her head under Ruby's chin.

"Jennie, that's what love is. When you would rather hurt than see them hurting, when you would brave your worst fear for them; that's love."

"My worst fear is marrying a man and then finding he's just like Pa."

226

Ruby brushed the hair from Jennie's eyes and stroked it back into her bun. "Do you really think Aiden has hidden who he *really* is from you? Do you honestly think he could be hiding something that dark from all of us?"

She thought about all the times he'd teased her and challenged her and infuriated her, but not once had he intentionally hurt her. Even when he'd said something that had cut her deeply, he'd told her she'd been mistaken and explained himself.

"He's been talking about courting you almost from the start, Jennie. He felt something between you as soon as you met. Beau wasn't ready to give him permission right away, but after he saw you two together the day you gave Aiden his shave... Beau told me he would approve if Aiden ever decided to ask again. He didn't until we got here, though. Why is that?"

Jennie flung her head into her hands and sobbed. "I told him not to. I didn't even know he'd still gone to Beau. If he was leaving and never coming back, I didn't want to be stuck here loving someone I'd never see again."

"You pushed him away at every turn. Don't you see now that if you'd taken the time to let him court you while you had the chance you could've gone with him to Kansas as his wife? You could've met the family that's so important to

227

him he's willing to leave the woman he loves for them. You could have been the great treasure he promised them."

Jennie let Ruby's words wash over her heart. She refused to believe them until he professed his love himself.

"But I didn't want to." Jennie wiped the back of her hand across her eyes. "I don't want to leave my family. We've already lost Ma and Hattie. I'm not splitting us up any more. Even you said, on our way to Deadwood, losing just one of us would be difficult. Why are you so ready to see me go now?"

"Jennie. Don't you see? Families may grow apart and live in other places, but that doesn't mean they love each other any less. I lived away from all of you for over a year and my love for all of you only grew stronger." Ruby touched her knee and Jennie glanced up to meet her gaze. "And it isn't like you'd never come back. Aiden wants to be here.

"You could write to Ma any time you wish. I have the address in my Bible. If you'd go with Aiden, you'd never be farther away than a letter, and now that they have the train in Deadwood, you could always visit."

"A letter..." Why hadn't she thought of that? She didn't have to lose him at all! "Aiden could write his parents a letter instead of going!"

Ruby grabbed and held fast to Jennie's hands. "Don't be disappointed if he still wants to go, Jennie. He knows his family better than you do. While it may seem to be the perfect solution, maybe he feels he *has* to go, because something important is waiting for him there. If you love him, you have to let him lead, and that might mean letting him go."

Her shoulders sunk. "None of that will matter if he dies."

A loud holler came from Ruby's room followed by Brody yelling instructions to Lei and Beau. Jennie sprang to her feet and Ruby clutched her hand tightly.

"Brody said no. You stay right here."

"He needs me, Ruby."

Ruby glanced at Jennie. "I think you'd best put together a pallet for Beau and me out here. It'll keep you busy. I don't think we'll be sleeping in there for some time."

Jennie sighed then nodded as she glanced back at the bedroom door one last time. "I best do that so I can keep my mind off what's going on in there. At least if he's yelling, he's still alive."

Chapter Eighteen

Aiden felt a cool cloth wipe over his brow and he heard... *humming*. He recognized it as a hymn but the more he tried to name it, the more he couldn't string two thoughts together. It didn't help that the pounding in his head was worse than the night the prospector introduced him to whiskey.

He opened his eyes and glanced around, squinting at the searing light pouring in the one window. Nothing looked familiar, until his glance fell on beautiful violet eyes smiling down at him. His left shoulder throbbed and he couldn't even think about moving it. He reached up with his other hand and wrapped it around the back of Jennie's neck. She slid down to her knees on the

KARI TRUMBO

floor, nearer to him. He pulled her closer and she did not protest as he claimed her lips.

Energy surged through him and he drew her tightly to him. She couldn't get close enough. Pain throbbed down his arm and she pulled away, laying her beautiful head on his chest. He let his hand rest against her neck holding her0, his fingers tracing the soft wisps of hair at her nape.

"Aiden, I'm so glad you're awake. I was so scared."

He moved his hand to her head and relished the feeling of her against him. "You can't get rid of me that easy."

She laughed and sat up, running the cool cloth over his forehead again. "You've had a fever. We were so worried about you. You're still so hot..."

He cupped her cheek and she closed her eyes. "I don't want to leave you behind, Jennie. Please say you'll come with me."

She shook her head as she pulled back, and a wavering smile covered her lips. "We could write them a letter, Aiden. I could even write it for you, now. You don't ever have to leave." She waited with expectant eyes for something he could never give her. And it broke him.

He trailed his thumb in circles in the soft hair by her ear. "I'm so sorry, Jennie. It can't be that way. I *have* to go. I won't be able to sleep easy until I go back and tell my folks how sorry I am. You can't do that in a letter."

Her face crumpled with a swallowed sob and her eyes shut tight against her tears. "I almost lost you once, please, don't make me lose you again." She leaned into his hand, letting the tears drip down her cheek and onto his thin undershirt.

"You don't have to lose anything. Don't you see? If you come with me, we'll always be together."

She shook her head, dislodging his hand from her hair, and he let it drop. "No, I can't go knowing I may never come back. And if you decide to stay, I can't come back alone."

"You'd do that? You'd rather be with your family forever even if it meant you wouldn't be with me?" His chest tightened as he waited for her to meet his gaze.

"I could ask you the same question and I'd think we'd both answer that it isn't like that. I *can't* leave them. Over the last half-year, everything I've ever known has changed. The only thing that's stayed the same are my sisters. Hattie has already done enough damage. I can't leave my sisters, too. If you go and I stay, then I hope you'll be more likely to come back."

He closed his eyes and saw that she

was right. They both needed their families for different reasons. She'd been here next to him while he'd recovered. That was *something*. But, what if *his* family didn't understand? What if they wanted him to work to make up for leaving them? Or, it was possible they didn't miss him at all. The pain would be great, but then he could come right back, but not as the man he hoped to be.

Fabric whispered next to him as Jennie stood. Her cool lips pressed against his head. He sighed and when he opened his eyes, he was alone. Whose bed was he in and how long had he been there? Had they found who'd shot him or was the scoundrel still on the loose? Brody came through the door and pulled up a chair.

"You've been down for quite a while. That little gal out there got a few gray hairs on account of you."

Aiden rubbed his shoulder and flinched. "I didn't sign up for this when I offered to go with Beau."

"You surely didn't. I got a good look at him. He didn't even bother to hide. Pretty sure he thought you were me, since you were riding one of my horses and we're about the same size." He shook his head. "I rode back to Lead and got the sheriff. He didn't want to take my word for it, but Beau was able to get a good look at him as well. He gave a description to the sheriff that closely re-sembled my neighbor, Jed. It was enough. Maybe we'll find out why he took a shot at you when the circuit judge comes through."

Aiden nodded. "So, when will I be able to get up and start earning my keep again? I have to get to Kansas so I can make good with my family. Then I can come back."

"You sound surer of your return now than you were before."

"I am. If I explain to my family I have a gal waiting here and she's more pre-cious to me than gold... I think they'll send me back."

"Well, just remember, if they don't, you send a letter. Don't leave that gal waiting on you. It wouldn't be right." He patted Aiden on his good shoulder then went around the bed to check the band-ages on his other. He made contempla-tive noises as he poked around.

"Yup, all the angry red around the wound is finally turning pink and puck-ering. The wound has scaled over well and isn't draining anymore. I think you'll keep your arm."

Aiden sat up and stared at Brody. Was he serious?

"I'm just funning with ya. There was never a question. I was an army medic with Custer. I got injured before the battle of Greasy Grass and was sent home as soon as my injury healed enough. You aren't the first bullet wound I've tended." He pulled the blanket up over Aiden and stood. "Glad to see you awake. I'll send Jennie back in here with a little soup, then I think Beau should help you up so Ruby and Jennie can freshen this room. Then you can rest. Beau has set aside the money for you to go as soon as you're well enough. When I see you not only awake, but walking around, we can talk about getting you a ride to town."

Aiden nodded. Brody didn't seem like the kind that would take well to taking orders, even in the army. He laid back against the wall as Brody left, letting his eyelids close while he waited. Unless the soup was already made, he'd have to wait a while for it anyway. The smell of old bandages, waste, and uncleanliness filled his nose. He hadn't been aware of it until Brody mentioned cleaning the room. He'd been too full of Jennie to notice. Now that she was gone, the stench wouldn't leave him.

Aiden shifted to get off the bed and stopped as pain tore through his arm. He held it close to his body and used his other side to pull himself to the edge of the bed. He pushed the covers off and realized they'd taken off everything but his drawers and thin undershirt. The door handle clicked and he swung the blankets back over himself wafting the stench into his face. It was enough to make his stomach curl.

"Jennie. I can't eat in here. I'm powerful hungry, but if I eat in here, it won't stay down."

"I don't blame you." The side of her mouth slid up and a mischievous twinkle lit her eyes. "I'll take this back out to the table and come back to help you up."

"No!" He shook his head. "I can't have you help me get dressed."

She laughed and a sweet pink tinge rimmed her ears. "Fair enough. Beau is home for lunch. I'll have him come in and help you." She swept out of the room and Aiden sighed.

Beau laughed as he came in. "I'm not sure what's funnier, that she just got you good or that you believed it."

Aiden frowned. "You shouldn't mock an injured man. Not a fair fight."

Beau put one hand under Aiden's right arm, the other under his elbow. "Jennie got your clothes cleaned and patched a week ago, though your coat was pretty well ruined."

"I'm sorry to hear that. The longer I stay with you, the more clothes I lose."

Beau led him over to the chair. Aiden sat and got to work putting on his own dungarees. He slid on a clean cotton under shirt to replace the one he'd been wearing and put his arm through one

236

sleeve of a clean shirt and draped the other over his shoulder on the other side, leaving it open for movement.

"That's good. Let's get you out of this room." Beau helped him to his feet once again and he pushed one foot in front of the other, moving his upper half as little as possible. Jennie waited at the table for him, she let her eyes roam over him possessively and he couldn't say he minded. He sat next to her and she pushed the bowl over to him. It warmed him to know that she understood he'd want to feed himself.

He lifted the spoon to his mouth and the soup was as sweet as honey to his tongue. Being without for so long made him appreciate the richness of the meal. He let the broth and vegetables sit in his mouth for a second, enjoying every bit of the flavor, then he swallowed slowly. His throat protested and he reached for a glass of water. The cool water trickled down after the scratchy food.

Beau sat across from him. "Aiden. I'm not sure if anyone said anything yet, but my pay was more than we needed with our food included. I put the money aside for you. As soon as you can, you'll be able to go home. There should be enough there for your return trip, too."

Aiden nodded and set his spoon down, reaching for Jennie's hand. "I want very much to go and do what's right, and pray I can return." He lifted

her hand and gently kissed Jennie's
knuckles.

Chapter Nineteen

Jennie stood on the porch as Aiden strode to the wagon and tossed his satchel in the back. A great fissure cracked her heart wide. His good arm reached for the seat of the wagon and lifted his leg to climb up. He was leaving and though he said he'd come back, what if he didn't? Could she really live with him never knowing just how she felt?

"No!" Jennie yelled and tore away from Ruby's grasp on her shoulder. Aiden turned and brought both feet back to the ground. He opened his arms for her. She ran to those welcoming arms and he lifted her right off the ground with his one good arm. Jennie folded herself around his neck and clung to him, her chest burning with tears. He pressed his lips to hers in a kiss that claimed her very soul, sweeping every ache into her center then exploding outward claiming all that was her as his own. His lips told her more than his words. He would return for her.

Slowly, he let her slide down until her feet touched the ground, but she didn't let go, couldn't let go.

"You'll take care of Jack for me?" He rested his head against hers and cupped her cheek.

She covered his hand and let her tears stream over them. She didn't want him to think of her as weak, but inside, the pain crushed her.

She nodded. "I will."

"You'll take care of my best girl?" Aiden murmured to the dog.

She raised her gaze to meet his. It immediately destroyed her resolve not to beg. "Oh, Aiden. Don't go."

"I promise I'll be back, Jennie-girl. M'fhíorghrá."

"You'd better." She held his hands over her face for a moment longer, then let him go. He gently pulled her into another tender kiss then turned and climbed into the wagon. Brody reined the horses into a trot and Aiden turned and waved to her. She raised her arm and watched until he was out of sight, then ran into the house and up into the loft. Her insides were as empty as a rain barrel in the desert. She lay on her bed and wrapped her arms around herself, holding on as tight as she could.

Eva rushed in after her and climbed onto the bed. "He'll come back, Jennie. He will. He promised."

"I know. But he's leaving... My heart is riding away from me and I wasted so much time worrying."

Eva rubbed her arm. "Be thankful you discovered your feelings before he left. How many women gave up their men to war, thinking they'd come back? It's okay to be sad, but if you mourn too long you'll only make the waiting all the longer."

Eva climbed off the bed and left the room. Jennie wiped her eyes. If she hadn't realized what Ruby said was true, Aiden might not have cared to ever come back. If he'd thought he had no chance, he may have stayed away. She'd come so close to losing him. Jennie sat up on the bed and went to her writing desk.

Dear Ma,
I know it's been some time since I've written to you, but there are things I want to talk to you about. I miss you so much. I've met someone who has me tied up in knots.
His name is Aiden Bradly and

he's a little older than me. He used to be a miner, but is now helping Beau on a ranch outside of Deadwood. Someone shot him and I thought I'd lose him. Until that happened, I knew I felt something for him, but it wasn't until I thought I'd lose him that I knew—

Jennie paused, holding the pencil above her paper. *Knew what?* She thought she loved him, but did she really? Ruby's words and even Eva's were a balm, but she needed her mother.

She continued:

...that I love him. There, I said it. But I need you, so much. I'm so confused.

I miss you so very much and need your guidance. We all need you. I know Ruby told you Hattie ran off, but we feel so torn. I know I'm asking a lot, but if you could come just for a visit, I think it would help. I don't understand what my heart's telling me and I'm so worried I'll make a foolish choice.

Sincerely Yours, Jennie

She read the letter over again. It was very short for the cost of a stamp, but what she really wanted, what she'd always wanted, was Ma with them. Ma had

242

always held the family together and she could fix it now. She folded the letter and put it in an envelope, taking care to write the name and address as clearly as possible.

Ruby climbed the ladder and sat on the chair next to the bed Jennie shared with the youngest two sisters. "I'm a little surprised at you, Jennie. We've seen Aiden hold your hand or maybe give you a small peck, but that was quite a display for your sisters.

"Because Ma and Pa were very private, Beau and I have tried to keep our affection under wraps. We don't always succeed, but we don't want them feeling uncomfortable with us."

Jennie turned to hide her discomfort. She'd felt what Ruby was hinting at when she'd caught Beau and Ruby kissing. She twisted her apron in her hands. "There's nothing wrong with what I did, Ruby. I'll miss him and I don't regret one thing."

"You didn't let me finish. I was going to say, perhaps it would be good for the younger girls to see more affection between Beau and I, so when they reach your age we don't have the same issues with them that you and Hattie have struggled with."

"Hattie... I wrote to Ma about her. I even asked her to come." She glanced at Ruby to see what she'd think. Ruby probably wouldn't stop her, but she should have asked permission first.

"Jennie. Do you really think she will? She was so enamored with Carlton, I don't think she'll come out here. She raised you girls the best she could and she was worn out after protecting you from Pa and his anger for so long."

Jennie let her shoulders fall. "I don't know if she'll come or not, but she won't if we don't ask." Jennie knotted her hands together in her lap. "What'll I do if he doesn't return?"

Ruby smiled and laid her hand over Jennie's. "You'll go on, just as you did before you knew him. Your life will be different, for sure, but you'll move on because you must."

"Did Beau say how long it would take him to get to Kansas?"

"I think he said it would take about five days. It's slow going through the hills. The rails can't travel any faster than fifteen miles per hour, not much faster than a horse and carriage."

Jennie sighed and tapped her pencil against her desk. "I've never ridden a train. I just thought it would be... *better.*"

"Trains will get better and faster. You'll see. In the meantime, I wouldn't expect Aiden back before a month. In that time, you can sew up some lovely dresses and start making things for when he returns and for the home you can make together. If he stays here, and you marry him, you may have to live with him in that tiny cabin. At least until he can buy land and build you something else."

"I don't care where we live as long as he doesn't have to leave again."

"That's another thing you need to think about. What if he only comes back to collect you and whisk you back to Kansas? Or, like mail-order brides, perhaps he'll just wire money for a ticket and have you meet him there."

"I told him I don't want to go."

"Why ever not? You don't even like Deadwood. You could have a fresh start."

"A fresh start far away from anyone I've ever known."

Ruby smiled. "Jennie, that's what a woman does. In fact, the good Lord built us to do just that, to leave our father and mother and cleave unto our spouse. He equipped women with the ability to make friends in almost any situation. You'll never be alone for long."

"But..."

"Stop making excuses. You'd best be ready for whatever happens."

Aiden watched from his seat in the third car of old #52 as the miles crawled by. He'd gone from hills and valleys, to more sharp lowlands where the railroad filled the area with rocks, gravel, and sand to make a straight path. Now the land was flattening out into prairie. A vast green sea opened in front of him and he couldn't quite tell where the green faded to blue to meet the sky. He sighed and slouched back into his seat. The ride had only been a little over a day, so far, and he couldn't shake the need to see Jennie. If he could turn the train back around, he would.

A small voice whispered *home* in his ear, but Kansas hadn't been home for a long time and he couldn't even be sure what he was going back to. Would his family even still be there? There was no way to know except to go. He'd already decided, as soon as he admitted to his parents that they were right, that he'd been foolish to leave, he would ask for their forgiveness. Then he'd head right back into town and get on the train. Nothing would keep him from running straight back into Jennie's arms.

The train squealed along the track. Just the day before, he'd gotten the worst headache of his life from that sound, but the longer he was forced to ride, the more he got used to it, as much as a man could. It was a little better if the window was closed, but only if all the windows near him were closed too, and that was rare. In the summer heat, everyone wanted the windows open for a breath of air, even if it meant the dust, smoke when they cleared the ash, and the awful whine of the wheels on the tracks came through the windows.

He thought about his older brother, Hugh. The good son. He'd always been there for Da and Mam. He'd done the work of two men when they were younger, and Aiden had always disliked him for it, holding a grudge. His brother tried to make him look bad, but now he knew that he'd just worked harder than Aiden. He'd been sure Da loved Hugh more. Now he knew that wasn't true. Hugh hadn't caused as much trouble as Aiden had. So, what appeared as more love was just less correction. He could see that now, looking back on his boyhood. If he'd known then what he knew now, that if he'd just minded his da, he never would've wanted to leave. He wouldn't have needed to. But then, he never would've met Jennie.

Aiden sat forward in his seat as if struck by a lightning bolt. If he hadn't been a wandering fool, and if the old prospector hadn't stolen his share, he never would've met the best thing that'd ever happened to him. He wove his fingers together and laid his head down in them. *Ok Lord. I see now. You can re-deem all situations. But what about this? What about with my parents?*

He gazed out the window as the train entered yet another small town and slowed to take on and let off passengers. He watched as men came home to waiting wives with children. They embraced on the platform outside his window. Happiness. Tears. If only that was waiting for him. He'd, yet again, been the bad son and could expect correction. A heaviness lay over his heart and he tried to shake it off without success. He reaffirmed his resolve to continue. If men ignored the hard tasks the Lord asked of them, perhaps He'd stop asking anything of them at all. No, he had to do this *because* it was difficult, to prove, at least to the Lord, that he could listen and obey.

Chapter Twenty

Jennie glanced behind her. No one followed her from the cabin. She needed to get out and away from the crush of people stuffed into the tiny space. She'd taken to wandering to Aiden's cabin and sitting outside it with Jack. Somehow, she felt closer to him near the cabin that had only been his for a short time. She sat on the ground, leaning against his door, and threw a stick for Jack to fetch. She turned her head to the sky as a giant rain drop splatted onto her nose.

She scrambled to her feet and rushed into the cabin. She hadn't set foot inside since Aiden had warned her not to enter a man's space. Even though he'd been gone for over two weeks, she could still smell the scent of his soap, the oil he used to clean the gun Brody had given him, and the fresh straw he'd filled his tick with before he'd left. She lay on the bed and held his pillow close to her, breathing deeply. A sob choked her. She closed her eyes and could see his face clearly.

The journal he'd found in the tiny servant's room at the house in Deadwood was now on a small table next to his bed. Curiosity overtook her as rain splashed against the windows. She flipped it open to a page on Pearson's first discovery of gold near what would eventually become the city of Deadwood in 1875. The following year, a few gunfighters attempted to clear out the gold rush riff-raff. John Reid would claim he'd civilized the town. Jennie laughed at the idea of a gunfighter civilizing anything.

Outside, the rain now came down in sheets and Jennie grabbed the flexibles from the mantle and lit Aiden's lantern so she could keep reading. In 1876, the town grew from 'a group of miners and riff-raff' to a platted town. At that point, the diary took on real life. Instead of blurry photos taken from a pinpoint camera, the writer had cut clippings from a newspaper. She traced the fine print with her finger as she read of Crazy Horse and Sitting Bull, the birth of the Deadwood's sister city, Lead, and how it grew from almost nothing overnight.

The book that Aiden had cherished enough to save linked her to him in a way she couldn't explain. And she read the pages as if she needed them to survive. She began to see why it had fascinated him so much. Deadwood had a rich history that wasn't all about gamblers, miners, and prostitutes, though they definitely had their roles.

She read how the *Deadwood Times,* the very paper Beau and Aiden had worked for, lobbied for a tax on prostitution to help clean up the city, and how much of the town burned to the ground in the fire of 1879. She sighed, closing the book and rubbing her eyes. She glanced out the window and realized she'd been there for hours. Ruby and everyone would be worried about her. She placed the book back where she'd found it and blew out the lantern.

Jack sat by the door and rushed out into the drizzle as soon as she opened it. Jennie held up her hand so she could see through the rain and picked her way over the puddles to her house. She said a little prayer that they had all stayed inside waiting for her, as there wasn't far she could go.

She pushed open the door and quickly closed it behind her, leaning against it.

Beau stood in the kitchen, his arms

crossed over his wide chest, his brow deeply furrowed. "Where can you have possibly been for the last few hours that you didn't hear Ruby and I calling for you?"

Jennie glanced down at her feet and felt the heat crawl up her face. "I was over at Aiden's cabin when it started to rain. I thought it would be over quickly, so I went inside to wait it out. Then it started pouring. I had nothing to do, so I was reading a book about Deadwood... and lost all track of time."

"You must've had a one-track mind. That cabin isn't more than twenty yards away."

"I'm sorry. I hope you didn't worry too much."

"Oh, we were worried, but not half as worried as your Ma."

Jennie's head snapped up and that's when she saw her mother, Maeve, standing behind Beau with a smile on her face.

"Ma!" She ran forward, pushing her way past Beau and into ma's waiting arms. "You came! But how did you get here so quickly? I only sent that letter two weeks ago?"

"The mail runs fast now that the trains carry it. I bought my ticket as soon as I got it and the train took a little over a week through the hills. If my daughter asks me to come, I come."

Maeve held her close. "Now, what's this I hear about Aiden Bradly?"

Ruby came forward and pulled out a chair for Ma. "Aiden is a young man we met on our way to Deadwood. He has steadily earned Beau's trust."

"It isn't Beau's trust I'm concerned with, it's how my daughter feels about this young man that matters."

Jennie sat down next to Ma. "He and I didn't get along at first. We were at odds, you could say. Then we found out he hurt his feet and I had to tend to him for a time. That's when he stopped teasing me so much and started talking to me."

Maeve laughed. "Men sometimes tease girls they like. Not cruelly, I mean, but they do."

"I was just starting to think about him more often when he told me he was going to up and leave as soon as he got the chance. Then, all I could think was that I wouldn't ever really matter to him... like you did to Pa."

Maeve reached out and took Jennie's hand in hers, then she glanced into the face of each daughter standing all around the table. "I want to tell you something, all of you. I loved your father for a time. Toward the end... he wasn't the same man I fell in love with. Love makes us blind to human faults, but know that if Aiden loves you, he's blind to yours, too."

Jennie watched as Ma shook her head, and the creases beside her eyes seemed to deepen. "About the time Hattie and Eva were born, he changed. He really thought that once we had a girl, we'd certainly have a boy. He went into a terrible rage and moved us out of Yellow Medicine, away from everyone. Two girls were more than enough, four was an outrage. He accused me of some terrible things, believed it couldn't be his fault we had girls. That's when loving him became hard."

Maeve pulled her hand away and rested her elbow on the table, cradling her head against it. "By the time Francis was born, he was out of money that he'd saved when he sold our house in town. He needed to find some way to make money or we'd all starve, so he built his first still. It wasn't long until all manner of men came to our door at all hours, looking for your father... and moonshine."

Ma closed her eyes and her forehead was deeply lined.

"I don't tell you all this to make you afraid of marriage. What I *would* tell you, is this: If I'd looked at who your father was before we were married, if I'd *really* looked at his character, I could've seen the man he would become. I let his charm blind me, and I was caught up in his fascination with me, and his kiss."

The younger girls giggled into their hands.

Jennie frowned. "But how? How do I look beyond the feelings? How do I know if I've found a good man?"

"When he hurts you, does he give a hollow apology or none at all, and does he do the same things again anyway?"

"No, not at all."

"That's good. I also like that Beau trusts him." She glanced at Ruby. "Despite what I said earlier." She smiled up at Beau. "Men don't usually feel the need to hide who they are from other men, so if Beau trusts him then Aiden most likely has hidden nothing from you. But lastly, I want him to pass the mother test. I talked to Mr. Ferguson on the ride here and he's agreed to let me stay in the big house until Aiden comes back. If I like him, I'll give my blessing and I'll return to Cutter's Creek after you're married."

Ruby sighed. "That's wonderful, but what about Hattie?"

Maeve shook her head. "Hattie's had her own demon for a long time, longer than any of you know. She'll come home when she's ready. Even if you find her, it has to be when she's ready or you'll push her further away. Ah, my girls. It's so good to see you. I've missed all of you these last months and I can't wait to tell you all that's happened with me. But first, we should eat our supper and get a rest. It's getting late."

Jennie gasped. "You didn't eat? I'm so sorry for holding you up."

Ruby stood and rested her hands atop Jennie's shoulders. "We all need a break from the walls sometimes, Jennie, just let me know before you fly away next time."

Chapter Twenty-One

Having just finished her chores, it was time to spend the afternoon with Ma on the couch in the small parlor of their cabin. She sucked in a deep breath as she searched through the large stack of fabric before her.

Maeve touched a white linen. "What a generous thing for Mr. Ferguson to do."

Jennie smiled. "I wasn't expecting all this, that's for sure. He said it had been stored in his mother's cabin and he found it after she passed."

Maeve opened and measured a white cotton against her arm. "These will make some lovely sheets for your bed."

Jennie glanced at the floor. "Yes, well..."

Maeve laughed. "Let me tell you what's been happening with me the last few months. Carlton and I have become dear friends. We attended a few weddings and a summer barn dance together."

Jennie eyed her mother. Carlton Williams could barely walk, dancing would be out of the question.

"I see you looking at me like I'm lying. I said we went, I never said we danced. We aren't like that, anyway. Carlton gets weak some days. His daughter is there to care for him since their housekeeper, Ivy, left last winter, but I do hope Aiden returns quickly so I can rejoin him. Carol isn't one for being a nurturer."

Jennie glanced out the window behind them. "I hope he returns soon, too."

"Let's get started on your hope chest. You're getting a late start. I never thought I'd be helping any of my daughters put one together. I'm so happy I could be here."

"I'm afraid the other girls will be jealous if you don't come back for them, too."

Maeve held her needle up to the light and threaded it, running the thread all the way to the other end and tying it off. "That'll be a while. I don't think Hattie is destined for marriage, at least not now, and though she and Eva are twins, she still acts quite young. But I would like, once Carlton is gone, to come here to stay with you. I didn't think it would be quite so lovely or as nice as Montana."

Jennie picked up a soft flannel and rubbed the light fleece fabric against her cheek. "I didn't want to live here at first. I missed Cutter's Creek, and you. I didn't think I'd ever like it, but the longer I'm here, the more I can't imagine ever leaving. It's more than just that my sisters are here now, it's like the Dakota's are part of me. The Sioux called this land the Paha Sapa; their holy lands. I can see how they think that. The land, the air, the water, it all gets inside you."

Maeve nodded as she whip-stitched the edges of a sheet. "I believe it and I also believe with all my heart that all my girls will find happiness here, even my wayward child."

"It isn't your fault, Ma."

One side of Maeve's mouth turned down. "There're only so many places you can seat blame. Hattie should never have had to learn to escape her own life, but she did. She did because of *my* choice to be with the man I'd chosen."

Maeve draped the fabric out over her and sighed deeply, her glance darted from Jennie back to the fabric. "Just be sure to make room for me, wherever you call home. I need to be with Carlton for now, but I'll be alone once he's gone. His daughter, Carol, is sweet now, but I don't see her welcoming me forever. I'm sure she and her husband will start a family of their own soon and fill that big house."

"Won't you want to stay with Ruby and the girls?" Jennie laid out the flannel to cut pieces for some sleeping gowns.

"Not if they're still in this house. I'd feel as if I was intruding here. I suppose I could ask Mr. Ferguson if I could live with him in his large house." She laughed. "I doubt he and his housekeeper would mind."

Jennie smiled. "I guess we'll ford that river when we get to it. You aren't yet ready to move her permanently."

"No, I'm not, but at least there's a lot I can do in the short time I'll be here."

Chapter Twenty-Two

Aiden tossed his pack over his shoulder and nodded to people he'd briefly met as he climbed off the train. The little town of Belvue was an hour's walk—if he couldn't find anyone headed that way to ride with. He shifted his hat and glanced around. Women in colorful walking dresses waved to one another in the street. Men chatted on the corners or carried loads as they did their work. Dust rose from the street as wagons, horses, and men went about their day.

The easiest way to find a ride would be to start walking and see who came along. He smiled and nodded to anyone who managed to catch his eye as he made his way west to the edge of town.

The open prairie spread before him with a rope of worn dirt for a road. After about twenty minutes of dragging his feet down the roadside, a wagon came up behind him.

"Ho there! You headed for Belvue?"

Aiden nodded. "All the way, if you go that far."

The man moved over on the seat and Aiden tossed his pack in the back and climbed up.

"Not many people visit Belvue, going to see someone?" He flicked the lines and the swayback old mares plodded forward.

"Yeah, I'm going home. Name's Bradly, Aiden Bradly."

"Well, if it ain't..." He laughed. "Your pa been talking about you for a year. He had an accident last winter though, ain't been the same since."

Aiden's gut tightened. "Is he all right?" He held his breath, waiting for the man's reply. It had been almost two months since he'd decided to come home, but even before then, his da had needed him.

"As all right as he *can* be. Crushed part of his back. He don't work no more. Walks with a cane."

Aiden's head sagged between his shoulders and his anger with himself burned hot. He should've been there. "I'm sorry to hear that. Are Hugh and

262

Peader still there helping him?"

The old man brushed his chin with his leather-gloved hand. "Hugh is, but not Peader. He was with your pa when the accident happened. He tried to save your pa by pushing him out of the way of a rolling wagon piled high with flour. They were both hurt, but Peader had gangrene set into his leg. They tried to take it, but he never beat the infection. I'm sorry."

Horror and grief collided within Aiden. He'd been selfish and run off then tried to justify it because he'd met Jennie. He shook his head. He'd have to see the state of the farm when he got there. Leaving to return to Jennie may be impossible. Jennie felt an ocean away and moving further by the second.

"Sir. Why don't you drop me off at the edge of town? I think I need a walk."

"Now son, this wasn't your doing. You can't get down on anyone. Bad things happen, that's just the way of it. It would've happened just the same if you'd been here or not, 'cept it might've been you that yanked your father out of the way. Then you'd be cold in your grave. Things work the way they do for a reason. It ain't your place to ask why, just how."

"What do you mean? What's the difference?"

The old man gazed over the vast prairie dotted with small houses. "Big difference. If you get stuck wondering why, you end up missing it. If you ask how the good Lord can use the change, well, then you're getting somewhere."

"I don't see how this can serve the Lord. I got a gal waiting for me back in South Dakota and if my family needs me, I may never see her again." He felt his blood rage in his veins. His brother was gone forever and he hadn't even known, because his family hadn't known where he was to send him a letter about it.

"Well, if she don't love you enough to understand, then maybe she ain't the woman you thought she was."

"But her family's there too, and they mean a lot to her. How can I make her choose my family over hers?"

"You haven't even been out to see your family yet and you're making plans. Maybe they don't want you there. Maybe they're so used to just living day to day that they can be just fine without you... or maybe your brother is tired. Maybe he's ready to sell out to a pushy ranch owner who's ready to give them a hunk of cash. Maybe you're here to convince them to move on. You don't know why you're here yet."

"Someone wants our land?"

"Yup. Paul Turbin."

Aiden watched as his own driveway touched the horizon ahead of them. The old man pulled up on the lines and held out his hand. "I wish you luck, Aiden Bradly. Pray and listen."

Aiden climbed down the side of the wagon and grabbed his pack. "Thank you. I'll do that. Wait, I didn't get your name?" The old man waved and turned back, the squeak of the wheels and the jangle of the traces continued down the road.

Each step was familiar, each large rock embedded into the ground brought back memories of running down the worn trail on the way to and from school. Hugh had never raced. He'd been too old for such fun, but he and Peader had. Peader. The loss hit him hard in the gut and he stopped. The farm held so many memories.

"I should have written... Then they could've told me." He kicked a stone off the path. "I don't deserve to even eat a meal with them."

He cleared the slight rise and his home lay before him. An old barn sat to the side of the house and newer machine shed lay beyond that. Someone sat on the porch on the old rocking chair. He stood and Aiden recognized Da, although he was now stooped and his once bright red hair was white. He slowly made his way off the porch and toward Aiden.

He'd been worried about this moment for two months and now it was here. His da could curse him and tell him to leave and never come back. Aiden wanted to get the confrontation over but he had to apologize before his da had a chance to say anything. Then, maybe, there'd be a chance at forgiveness.

Da stopped a few steps from him, his face flushed and hands shaking. Aiden waited. Da held out his shriveled arms and looked Aiden in the eye with all the pain of a man who'd had everything but life taken from him. "My son."

Aiden rushed to his da and embraced him. "I'm so sorry, Da. You were right, about everything. I was a fool. I should've stayed."

His da grasped his shoulders in hands that were surprisingly strong. "None of that matters. You're home. Come, your mam will want to see you right away."

Aiden tossed his bag back over his shoulder and followed, feeling for the first time like an outsider on the land he'd grown up on. His mam rushed from the house, then gathered her skirts in her fists to run and meet them. He caught her in his arms and held her tight. When he released her, she cupped his face in her hands as a tear ran down her weathered cheek.

"Is it really true? Are you really home?" She reached for her apron to wipe the tears from her eyes.

"I'm back," he said, wishing he could tell them everything. Their joy at his arrival was so strong he couldn't bring himself to tell them about Jennie. Would they hate her for taking him from them again?

"Come. I've got supper on the table. Hugh will be so glad to have help again."

They walked with him to the house and opened the door. His chest clenched at the sight. The house hadn't changed at all. Ma's patchwork quilt lay folded neatly on the back of the old couch. Under that quilt was woodwork that he and Peader had carved up when they'd gotten their first knives... and gotten a tanning shortly after. The fireplace was as clean as mam always kept it with the smell of bread baking in a hanging pot inside. Not once had they run out of bread as children. He could count on a thick warm slice any time he'd been hungry. His stomach rumbled at the thought and mam clapped him on the shoulder and laughed. He winced and rubbed the still sore wound.

"What happened?" Da asked?

"I was shot. I was working for a cattle rancher near Deadwood and his neighbor wanted more than his share. I got in the way." Aiden tugged at the shoulder of his vest to cover the spot. He didn't even want to talk about Deadwood, it would lead to too many questions.

Hugh strode into the house and stared at him for a moment, then turned to wash his hands, black with oil from working. "So, the favorite son returns. Did you bring us the famed *largest gold nugget you've ever seen, dearthái*r? Did you come bringing anything but another mouth for me to feed?"

Da jabbed his cane into the floor and growled. "Enough! I'll not have fighting. This is a day of rejoicing! My son is home!"

"Forgive me da, for not joining in your celebration. The threshing team that was supposed to be here next week has been held up by the weather further south. From their telegram, they're at least a week behind. If the rains come, they won't be able to get into the field at all."

Aiden shifted in his seat. "Why don't we use the old thresher. We could get it done together."

Hugh arched an eyebrow. "You hardly lifted a finger to help when you lived here. There's no way I'm going through the work of getting everything up and working, just to discover it's too much for you. That'd be a waste of time."

Da held up his hand. "It's time to eat. Your mam has worked hard to prepare us a good meal, let's not spoil it."

The four of them sat at the table but

his mam placed an extra plate where Peader used to sit. She held the plate for an extra moment, then shook her head and went back to bringing the food to the table.

Da sat at the same seat he'd always occupied. "Since you haven't asked, I'll guess someone told you about Peader."

"Yes. An old man gave me a ride to Belvue and as soon as he found out who I was he told me what happened. He also told me about Paul Turbin." Aiden glanced at Hugh to gauge his brother's thoughts.

Hugh shook his head. "I want to finish the harvest... after that... I make no guarantees. This isn't family land. We've lived here one generation. The rest of our family are still in New York."

"Do you want to go back there?" Aiden couldn't understand why Hugh would even consider going back. They'd left for a reason.

Da knocked his cane against the floor. "No. I won't go back. I don't have the strength to help Hugh anymore, Aiden, but you do. You can save the farm from Turbin's clutches."

Aiden sighed and scooped some turnips onto his plate.

"What's the matter? Now that you're here, you don't want to commit to work? Just like it used to be." Hugh sneered.

Aiden slammed his hand down on the table. "You don't know what my last year has been like."

Hugh narrowed his eyes. "And you don't know what it's been like here, because you left and never bothered to tell us where you were." He leaned back in his seat and crossed his arms over his chest. "So, you said you got shot up working on a ranch near Deadwood, isn't that where they found gold a few years back? Not surprised you'd be there. Did you get shot protecting a claim? Prospectors are miserable low-life's who'd just as soon steal from you as they would work." He spat the words at Aiden.

Aiden shot to his feet. His brother only knew one prospector, him, so the slight hit home. "You shouldn't talk about what you don't know and will never understand."

"Are you challenging me, little brother?" Hugh stood and leveraged his hands on the table, leaning forward and staring at Aiden.

His brother had at least forty pounds on him and a few inches, but anger could take you a long way. "Yeah, I guess I am." Aiden leaned forward toward Hugh, his muscles tense and ready.

Mam slammed her spoon down on the table. "Boys! You mind yourselves at my table. I'll not have you two throwing your muscles around here. Eat your supper then take it outside."

Aiden sat down. "Yes, Mam."

Hugh scowled at him. "After we eat, brother."

Chapter Twenty-Three

Aiden massaged the sore muscles of his hands. Throwing hay was a lot different than throwing an axe, but he wouldn't slow down. He couldn't, not with Hugh dogging him at every turn. He'd been back for a little over a week and, though his body was sore from the work, the field was in before the threshing team had even come to town. It had been long hours in the hot sun but his brother hadn't said a word, so at least supper time was quiet.

He strode into the barn and over to the horse he'd been riding, Sol.

"So, the favorite son finally appears. Day starts at sunup, brother." Hugh tossed a saddle blanket at him.

"Cut the *favorite son* nonsense. We

both know it was *you* da favored."

"How dare you come back here after being gone so long? All I heard for a year was moaning about the son that left. What about the sons who worked day in and day out to make the farm work? One of those sons gave his *life* for this place, but it never mattered since you were gone."

Aiden held his anger in check. He'd never been favored, had always been a breath away from the woodshed. Hugh would never know that humiliation. "He never loved me! I was always in trouble. I left so he'd never have to deal with me again, and so I could become a better man. I left so that when I came back with enough wealth that Da wouldn't have to work so hard he'd finally see *me*, not the oldest son who was trusted and would take over everything, not the youngest son who was allowed free rein, but as *me* the one who tried so hard to be seen at all that I would do *anything* for it. You don't get it. He praised you for everything." Aiden couldn't keep his voice in check. He slammed his hand against the wall and the tools hanging above his head shifted and clinked together.

Hugh turned his back on Aiden and leaned against the horse stall. "I wasn't allowed to play, even as a child. I was always in his shadow, always had to learn something new, and I had to do it right the first time. While you and Peader were out fishing, and having fun, I was learning how to plow, how to work."

"At least he showed you! I had to learn from you, from someone who hated me!"

"I never hated you! I wanted to *be* you! Until you came back, I had da convinced it was a good idea to sell to Turbin. I'm only thirty-three years old and I'm tired, Aiden. I want to be married, have a family... and I can't because I work all the time. I feel guilty if I take a day off. But if I don't do it, the work won't get done. This farm grew as we brothers did, so all three of us would help and prosper when we came of age, but I can't do the work of three anymore. I won't."

"Hugh, I never planned to saddle you with all this. I didn't leave to make you work harder."

"That may not have been your intent, but that's exactly what happened. I'm going over to Turbin's to try to get him to hold his offer. You try to convince Da that it's a good idea. If you don't succeed, I'm leaving anyway. We've got plenty of family in New York that would help me get on my feet."

Hugh mounted his horse and rode away. Aiden watched the open gate for a minute then turned at the sound of muffled footsteps behind him.

Mam folded her hands in front of her and regarded him with soft eyes. "Why do I get the feeling there's more to your story than what you told Hugh? You've been here only a few days, but I can tell you've changed. You yearn for something that isn't here." She laid her hand on his shoulder and the sadness in her eyes tore at his heart.

He didn't want to hurt Mam, but he ached for his Jennie. "Do you remember how you told us you and Da fell in love and decided to move away from your family to give your new family a better chance?"

"Of course, I do." Her face softened and she patted his shoulder gently.

"I met someone in Deadwood. Jennie Arnsby. She reminds me of you a little, the way her temper gets her sometimes, but mostly she's as sweet as can be. I miss her, Mam. I miss that girl so much it hurts."

"Why'd you come back, Aiden?" She pulled him over to some bales of straw and sat him down.

"I felt like I needed to. Like I had to tell Da that he was right and that I was sorry for the things I said and for leaving the way I did."

"You did that the very first thing when you got here. Colin told me it was so. But why didn't you tell us about this young woman? Didn't you think that would bring us even more joy? To see you happy and married? Da and I thought you came home because your fervor for that life had finally diminished."

"Mam, I'd like to take a little extra time and convince Da to listen to Hugh's plan. Then, I want you to think about coming back to Deadwood with me. I could build a house near the ranch where I work, big enough for you and Da, Rachel, me and Jennie."

"And all the grandkids, don't forget those!" She smiled and patted his leg.

"Do you think Da would consider it?"

"I think he will, but I worry about Hugh. He's had quite the burden this last year. I thought he'd be happy when you returned, but perhaps it was just too late. I'll talk to Colin for you, you can talk to Hugh. New York is not where he wants to be. My sisters and brothers still live in poverty." She closed her eyes. "He doesn't know what he wants, only that he wants away from here."

"I'll talk to him, Mam. But please, even if he chooses to go to New York, will you come with me to Deadwood?"

She crooked the side of her mouth. "I hope your bride and I get along."

Chapter Twenty-Four

Jennie scanned the stack of gowns, towels, sheets, night clothes, napkins, curtains, and other things laying on her side of the bed. It was all meant to go inside the beautiful cedar chest Beau had made for her.

The cedar bushes were all over the pastures, and Brody had asked Beau to remove them. He had, then he'd brought the thick trunks to the mill in Lead to be hewn down into boards.

Jennie ran her hand over the lacquered top. It was beautiful. She'd never owned anything like it.

Maeve slowly climbed the ladder and sat on the bed next to all the clothing. "I'm so sorry I couldn't be here long enough to meet your Aiden. I'll try not to think less of him for not returning right away so I could."

Jennie closed her eyes. "I hope we didn't work this hard for nothing. After the third week, I started to lose hope. Now it's been five weeks since he left and not even a note."

Maeve kissed the top of her head. "Dear, sweet Jennie. Don't lose hope. While it would've been nice if he'd written a letter telling you what was keeping him, we don't know what trials he's going through. I hope that you'll write me as soon as he does return."

"He has to come back first." Jennie lifted a few things and laid them gently in the chest, the scent of cedar a welcome change from the scent of the ranch.

"Don't worry. He *will* return, and then all these things will be ready to use. You'll see. Goodbye, dear. I'm getting a ride into Deadwood with Brody. He's quite a nice man, not as nice as Carlton, mind you, but nice." She stood and held out her arms.

Jennie stood and hugged her mother tightly. "Thank you. It meant so much to have you here. It would've been an endless five weeks without you."

"Yes, I'd think you'd have worn the pages near through on that Deadwood book of Aiden's." She winked.

Jennie smiled. "He told me to find

something I love about Deadwood, turns out what I loved was him."

Maeve nodded and swung down the ladder. She waved one last time as she closed the front door. Jennie sat back down on the bed and picked up one of the handkerchiefs she'd made for Aiden. She hadn't known his middle initial or even if he had one, so she'd embroidered it A.B. in pretty blue floss. The stitches were neat even though they'd worked quickly on each and every piece. Her sisters had even helped with a few of the less intimate items, like table cloths. Jennie touched the soft linen to her face then pulled it away as a tear fell. She didn't want to have to wash and press it again.

The sound of the wagon rolling away made her stand and go to the window. She'd searched the horizon every time she'd heard one for the last few weeks. This time it was her mother leaving, going home to Cutter's Creek. If she'd had her way back in late April, when they'd left, she never would've met Aiden. Many other things wouldn't have happened either, but meeting Aiden tempered the more painful things.

Slowly, she packed each item in the chest and closed the lid. Beau would have to bring it back downstairs, as she could barely lift it empty. Where he'd put it remained to be seen. If Aiden were back, they could just store it in his cabin. He wouldn't care to look inside it, so it would still be a gift when she opened it for him. But, she couldn't ask Beau to put it there before Aiden returned.

She climbed down the ladder and curled onto the couch. Beau and Ruby had lightened her chores with the amount of sewing she'd been doing with Ma, but now that she was gone, she'd get right back to her normal chores.

Soon, I'll have my own house and there'll be no one to help me with my chores. "But, only if he comes home," she muttered.

Jennie opened the Deadwood journal to a news clipping from September of 1879. *A fire erupted from an overturned kerosene lantern and quickly spread to a nearby hardware store where barrels of gunpowder exploded into a massive inferno that left over two thousand people without shelter.* Jennie read further and her eyes grew heavy. She moved to the rug in front of the fireplace and pulled a blanket over her, rubbing her eyes to stay awake. She didn't want to be found napping in the middle of the day, but Ma's departure had left her exhausted.

Flopping the book back open in front of her, she ran her hand down the column until she found her place and began reading more about the bakery where the fire began. The words merged together on the page and she stared into the fire in front of her. The flames burst in and out of focus. She felt as if the fire pulled her into its depths then shoved her out.

Her lids closed and when she opened them again, she was surrounded by fire. A towering inferno lay in front of her. It was the house from Deadwood.

She ran inside and the bright orange flames danced all around, singeing her skin and clothing. Something was inside the house, but the painful heat kept pushing her back. She slipped past the flames but they chased her back to Aiden's room. Instead of Aiden, Hattie was there, a shell of the girl she used to be. Hattie looked up at her, her eyes empty of emotion, her dress torn and tattered. She poured a bottle of alcohol onto the flames around her own bed and laughed. "You can't help me now. I'm too far gone."

Chapter Twenty-Five

Aiden's hands slipped on the side of the wagon. The closer he came to Jennie, the more he wanted to jump from the wagon and run. He had to see her. His heart beat erratically in his chest and his muscles wouldn't relax. Five weeks was five too many. He shook his hands, one at a time, to relieve the tension.

Colin elbowed his wife. "Martha, do you think the lad's nervous?"

She smiled back at him. "I'd say he is. He's never been good about writing letters, I'd bet he's worried what she'll think when he walks through the door."

His parents had always been able to read him well. He was just glad Hugh had decided to stay in Deadwood to find work, because Hugh would go out of his way to make Aiden even more nervous. Even after the evening they'd spent in the barn just before they'd left, he still knew how to rile Aiden. And enjoyed it. The wagon leaned as they started the trail around the hill up to the ranch house. Colin pitched to the side as the wagon tilted. Martha screamed and Aiden reached back and caught him before he fell out. His sore shoulder wrenched painfully, but he wouldn't say a word. Complaining would do nothing.

Colin laughed. "I managed the whole trip and now that we're here, I almost hurt myself."

Aiden could read the pain in his eyes. He'd been so strong before. It had to be hard to be reduced to shuffling around with a cane. Brody navigated the last turn up the hill and the house appeared before them. Aiden chuckled as his parents gasped over the site of the large house. His happiness was short-lived as Brody pulled the wagon to a stop. Aiden heard terrible screams of pain that made the hair on his arms stand on end. They were coming from Beau's cabin. Ruby ran from the barn toward their home and Aiden jumped from the bed of the wagon, making it to the door before Ruby.

He threw open the door to see Jennie reaching into the fireplace, the arms of her gown were alight and she was screaming. Her eyes were open, but un-seeing, as if she were blind.

Aiden ran to the fireplace and yanked her out, smothering her in his arms to put out the flames. He grabbed a blanket from the couch and wrapped it around her, hoping to kill any remaining embers. Jennie shook in his arms and he tilted her head up. Her vacant eyes stared at the ceiling above him.

"Jennie?" he kissed each of her eyes. He searched her face for some sign of recognition.

Ruby touched Jennie's shoulder. "Jennie?" She shook her and Jennie continued to look at the ceiling. Ruby picked up Jennie's scorched hand, already swelling and turning a bright pink. She led Aiden with Jennie to the table and brought over a pitcher of clean water. She dunked Jennie's hand in it and Jennie screamed, yanking it out.

Jennie looked down at her hands, then at Ruby. "What ... what happened?"

"Aiden pulled you out of the fire-place. I think you should tell *us* what happened."

"Aiden?" Jennie turned and her eyes locked onto his chest, then moved slowly up to his face, locking on his eyes. "You're home..."

"I am." He wrapped his arms around her. "I've never been so scared in all my days. I don't ever want to hear you scream like that again." He pulled her close to him and she shuddered and wrapped her arms around him, her tears wetting his shirt.

He kissed the top of her head. "I'm home to stay, Jennie-girl. In fact, I've brought my family with me, so neither of us has to sacrifice the love of our families to be together."

She backed away from him. "Oh, Aiden. You missed my mother! I waited and waited, but she had to leave earlier today."

"I didn't miss her. I saw Brody at the train station with a lovely lady and he introduced me to your mother, right before she boarded her train. I wish I'd been able to get back quicker, but there was a lot of work to do on the farm before we could sell it."

He reached for her wrists, avoiding the hands that were now swollen to twice their size. "I want you to soak those in cold water while I go take care of my parents. You'll get to meet them soon. Let Ruby take care of you. We'll all hear what happened after I get my parents settled so they can rest."

Jennie nodded and Ruby took her back into her room to see to the burns on Jennie's arms and hands. Aiden shook his head and glanced at the fireplace. If he'd gotten there any later, it may have caught her hair and the damage would've been much worse. Why would she stick her hands into the flames and what was wrong with her that she didn't see him? The questions weighed like rocks on him.

Martha waited next to the wagon. Colin had already gone inside with Brody.

"I hope whoever that was is all right now. I've never heard such a noise." She shuddered.

"Yes, she's fine now and her sister Ruby's taking care of her. I'll get you settled and you can meet Jennie tonight at supper. Does that sound good?"

Martha nodded. "That's fine. It's been a long journey. We haven't traveled so much since we came to Kansas. I'm ready for a rest."

Aiden put his hand at her waist and led her up to Brody's house, he opened the door for her and Mrs. Chen waited just inside.

"Mrs. Bradly?" Lei tilted her head.

"Yes, I am." Martha held out her hand.

Lei inspected her hand for a moment, then reached out and shook it. "Your Mr. Bradly is resting."

Aiden waited for his mother to go up-stairs, but as soon as they stepped out of his sight, he ran back outside and over to Beau's house. He didn't bother with knocking. Jennie couldn't wait.

His eyes filled with the sight of her

as he slammed the door open. She sat at the table holding out her arms, wearing only a chemise with her stays and a skirt. Both women jumped when the door hit the wall and Jennie moved to cover herself, but Ruby grabbed her upper arms and held them wide.

"You're covered enough. I need to get this salve on you right away or you'll scar. Stay put." Ruby glared back at him. "Aiden, I have a door for a reason. Kindly turn your back so I can get this done."

He blinked and forced his mouth closed. His beautiful Jennie was all shades of pink and red with harsh white lines around the reddest parts. He slowly turned away from her and his heart sunk. Would she be scarred? Did it matter?

"Jennie, while I finish wrapping your arms, why don't you tell Aiden and me what happened. Is it like when we were kids?"

Jennie's voice was soft. "Yes. I think so. I know I used to walk in my sleep and wake up in strange places. It hasn't happened for a long time, though."

"You used to sleep so deeply that you could walk around the house, eyes open, and we didn't know you weren't awake. None of us knew if there was something wrong with you or not, but then you grew out of it," said Ruby.

"I was reading the Deadwood book of

Aiden's, it was a journal someone had left behind. I was reading about a fire and Ma had just talked to me about Hattie. I guess my mind confused the two in my sleep. I remember seeing her in the house in Deadwood. She was in a huge fire and I wanted to save her, but she poured something on the flames and they erupted all around her. I tried to pull her out... and then I was standing in the kitchen with my hands in cold water. It hurts so bad." Jennie's voice shook and Aiden clenched his fists to keep from rushing over to comfort her.

"Aiden. Jennie is covered now, you can turn around," Ruby said.

Aiden spun and ran over to Jennie. He came behind her and wrapped his arms around her shoulders to avoid touching her burns. "If you walk in your sleep, we'll find some way to heat without fire. Something. When we're together, I'll protect you. I won't let this happen again."

Ruby stood up tall and slammed her hands to her hips. "Aiden Bradly, that might be the worst proposal I've ever heard. And don't you dare make another sound until you talk to Beau. You have to ask *him* first."

Aiden pegged her with a smile he felt right down to his toes and squeezed Jennie closer. "I don't have to do any such thing. I asked her mam when I met her at the train. She not only gave her blessing, she laid a kiss on my cheek for good luck."

Aiden came around to the front of Jennie's chair and knelt in front of her. He didn't want to hurt her hands so he laid them on her knees. "M'fhíorghrá, I promise to love you forever, will you marry me and love me, too?"

She lifted one of her bandaged hands and touched his cheek so gently. A timid smile touched her lips. "I will. I'll love you always, Aiden."

He laid his head in her lap and every fear he'd had of not measuring up lifted. He was himself, and that was more than enough for his Jennie.

"Now that's better." Ruby grumbled as she left them, closing the door softly behind her.

Six weeks later

Chapter Twenty-Six

Jennie sat in the back of the wagon with Colin as they drove down the peak of Ferguson hill. Colin poked her gently with his cane.

"The lad says you need to close your eyes." He laughed.

Jennie shook her head; used to his teasing at this point. Now she knew where Aiden got it. "I've been waiting for a month while he and Beau have been working. I can't close my eyes! I want to see it!"

He laughed harder. "Feeling cramped in that little cabin, eh? You should've seen the little place Martha and I had when we first moved. Not much more than two walls leaned in on one another."

Jennie's leg danced up and down as she nervously waited for the wagon to descend. At first, she'd been disappointed when Brody sold them the land at the base of the hill, the very edge of his property. They would live right off the road without any of the views the upper homes boasted. Then Aiden had brought her down and showed her the spot. The area at the base of the hill reminded her a little of Montana, and it was nestled in a small valley between three hills. Protected, sheltered.

They curved around the hill and she could see the roof. It was much bigger than she'd thought it would be. A two-story home with white painted boards and green trim. It had a porch big enough to sit on and Aiden had even planted some flowers along the front for her. Jennie couldn't speak. All the words she could think to say were trapped behind the lump in her throat.

Aiden came out of the house and closed the door behind him, beaming as the wagon came to a stop. He looked perfect, standing on the porch of their home. A feeling of peace and contentment washed over her. She'd never fear change again, not as long as they were together.

"Mrs. Bradly, what do you think of your new house?" He held his arms wide for her.

She jumped from the wagon and

rushed to him, throwing her arms around his neck. He lifted her and swung her around. "Let me show you the inside." He opened the door and led her in.

Jennie stood in a large living room, already furnished.

"I don't understand... Where did this furniture come from? It isn't new, but it isn't from the cabin." She turned to glance at him, then back at the couch covered with a hand sewn quilt.

"It was my parents'. They had it all shipped here when we moved. It's one of the things that took so long to arrange before we left. Hugh helped me move it out and get it set up."

"Hugh? I haven't seen him since the wedding. I thought he'd be gone to Lead by now."

Hugh appeared from the back room and touched his hat. He was so like Aiden, but darker and taller and so quiet. He hadn't said more than a handful of words to her since they'd returned. Where Aiden had the light red hair of his father. Hugh had his mother's dark hair. Even when he smiled, there was a brooding secret behind his eyes and he never laughed.

"Thank you, Hugh. Without your help, I would've had to wait even longer to be in my house." She squeezed Aiden closer and winked.

Hugh shook his head. "Aiden had to hurry or he would've missed my help. I'm headed to Lead this afternoon. I'll be there for a while. Bullock is sending me on a special job to find your Hattie. He thinks she's in Lead... and that she probably couldn't leave if she wanted to."

Jennie gasped and covered her mouth, then dropped her hands and hid them in the folds of her dress. They were still discolored from the burns and they embarrassed her to no end. She'd seen the doctor in Deadwood and he didn't know if they'd ever heal completely. Only time would tell. In the meantime, she covered them.

Aiden put his arm around her shoulder. "Godspeed, brother."

Hugh nodded. "I'll need all the help I can get." He tipped his hat. "I'll go help Mam and Da move their things in, then I'll be off. You probably won't see me for quite some time."

Hugh left and Jennie turned to Aiden and returned her hands to his neck.

"Thank you, Aiden. It's perfect."

"It wasn't perfect until you walked through the door. Now, it's home." Aiden leaned forward and tugged her down on the couch, onto his lap, kissing her until she felt it down to her toes.

As always, her heart soared. She drew back and cupped his cheek. "Aiden, I do believe you need a shave."

She laughed as his eyes grew wide with apprehension.

"I don't have two dollars, Jennie-girl." He gently twisted the hair by her ears, uncoiling it loose from her bun.

Jennie laughed and leaned forward, whispering in his ear, "I've never kissed a man fresh from a shave." She watched him scuttle to their room for his new shaving kit. She couldn't help but remember the shave she'd given him after she'd first met him, and how she'd wanted to kiss him even back then. But she hadn't; she'd been so afraid to live.

While Deadwood would never be Cutter's Creek, with Aiden by her side, it would always be home.

Historical Elements

Dreams in Deadwood takes place, of course, in Deadwood South Dakota, just three short years after South Dakota became a state. While the whole story is a work of fiction, I've done my best to include little bits of Deadwood history within the story. Here are a few examples:

The *Deadwood Times* mentioned in the story was actually called the *Deadwood Pioneer-Times*. The editor was known for showcasing areas he thought could be enriched within the city of Deadwood and was a big supporter of taxation on prostitution. You can find old issues online at https://www.news-papers.com/newspage/93970696/.

Deadwood began as a mining town, a western boomtown that practically grew up overnight. With mining towns, and the single men that worked them, came the gambling, saloons, and bawdy houses that the Old West is known for. At the time of this story, men quite literally outnumbered women 10 to 1, and wandering the street without a chaperone wouldn't have been recommended for a young woman.

This story takes place in 1892, just 15 short years after the Black Hills war,

also known as, the Great Sioux War of
1876. While fear of the Indians may not
have been forefront on people's minds,
it was close enough in history that the
fear was real. I tried to convey that by
mentioning it but not making it a main
focus of the book.

Seth Bullock would later become fa-
mous for his friendship with President
Theodore Roosevelt, but prior to that he
was known for taming Deadwood, or at
least giving it a good shot. Some would
claim Deadwood still isn't tamed. The
day after he arrived, the notorious Wild
Bill Hickock was shot and, because
Deadwood had little more than a camp
court at the time, his murderer went
free. For a time. Bullock deputized citi-
zens to help him and he was later sworn
in as sheriff. Would he have taken any
interest in a missing girl at the time? I
can't say, but I *can* say, judging by the
historical record, he probably would
have appointed Hugh to do the job.

The city itself has changed drasti-
cally over time. Deadwood has suffered
three major fires that decimated much
of the town. In fact, it was one of the
first towns in the west to enact building
codes requiring brick buildings, which
is why the old parts of Deadwood, if you
visit today, are all brick. Those are the
buildings that survived.

I'd like to take a moment to specially thank the Adams Museum and the Adams House in Deadwood, South Dakota for creating my fascination with Deadwood. I highly recommend a visit to these places on your next visit to Deadwood.

Sad to see it end? Join my mailing list to keep up-to-date on when the next Seven Brides of South Dakota book will be released! You can sign up at www.KariTrumbo.com

Kari Trumbo is an inspirational romance author, blogger and proud home schooling mother to four great kids. She interacts often on reader groups on Facebook and volunteers at the local library when needed. When she isn't writing, she is obsessively reading and expanding her skills as a wordsmith. Kari lives in her great-grandfather's remodeled 1890-built home in central Minnesota with her husband, children, cats, and one hungry wood stove.

Other Titles:

Western Vows

Forsaking All Others
To Honor and Cherish
For Richer or Poorer
To Love and Comfort

Cutter's Creek

A Lily Blooms
A Penny Shines
A Carol Plays
A Ruby Glows

Made in the USA
Lexington, KY
13 March 2017